THE CAVES OF ARKEH:NA
by Melissa Sweeney

ISBN 978-1-7338679-0-0 (pbk)

ISBN 978-1-7338679-1-7 (eBook)

Table of Contents

Chapter 1: The Arkeh:nen

As Avery hiked up the mountain home, the leaves from yesterday's storm tripped her up and slammed her into the mud. She reacted fast enough and saved herself from losing a tooth, but the Earth finally ripped up the last pair of clean leggings she owned.

At the sound of her fall, her two huskies, Oreo and Pumpkin, exploded with barks. They were in the garage up ahead, tied to the support beam so they couldn't get loose. They had enough leash length to sniff the edges of the unending forest, and their respective black and orange ears jumped behind the bushes outlining the property, eager to see their owner from school.

Avery wiped the mud off her leggings as she eyed her cabin home. Her parents had chosen this house to feel more "rustic," but it didn't fit the picture at all: tall, polished windows, decorated porches, and empty balconies. It only impressed their neighbors of squirrels and robins.

She stared through the curtained windows. She waited to see if her parents would come outside to the commotion, maybe see if she needed help.

Nobody came.

She fixed her beanie over her eyes, pet her dogs, and went inside.

Her mother was planted where she always was after school, at the dining table between mountains of work.

Her father was cooking in the kitchen. The familiar scent of their Friday dinner of herb chicken wafted through the first floor and grounded Avery back home.

When she closed the garage door, her father looked up. His glasses, fogged from cooking, slipped down his long nose. "Hey there. How was your first Friday of school?"

"Good," Avery said, but it wasn't. Sidestepping around her two hungry dogs, she pulled out their food dishes from the cabinets and divided their food can into two mushy piles. Pumpkin jumped and scratched the granite counter while Oreo waited patiently by her side. He'd gotten used to her feeding him. Pumpkin still thought Avery's mother and father would find the time to feed them.

After feeding them and cleaning out her lunch bag, Avery gave the dining room a quick nod—it looked like her mother nodded back—before she climbed up the stairs on her hands and knees to her loft.

She had the loft to herself, complete with a small bath and fireplace. Her bed lay unmade near the banister. Pictures of her from throughout the years snaked around the poles. From preschool to last spring, young Averys beamed up at the camera, holding frogs or flowers she thought looked pretty. This timeline had holes, though, missing pieces she'd ripped from her own memory. Those pictures were currently in a pile by her fireplace, ready to be burned.

She looked past the railing to the windows overlooking the Adirondack Mountains. Whenever she had a troubling day—like today, every day—she outlined the blurry mountaintops and waited for a line of geese to fly up to Canada.

But nothing beat backpacking down its trails and losing herself in the woodsy depths.

After her dogs gobbled up their food, Pumpkin scampered to the staircase and pawed the first step, waiting with her tail wagging.

Avery checked the Sun's position in the sky. She had three hours of daylight left.

She acted fast. She unhooked her hiking backpack from her closet and equipped it with two water bottles, her flashlight, her extra batteries, and her pocket knife. She switched out her tennis shoes for a pair of Timberlands and changed into a longer sweater. She didn't bother with her leggings now that they mirrored every other pant in her closet. Before leaving, she snatched her walkie-talkie from her mirror wardrobe. Her mother insisted that she carry one in case her phone ever lost signal and she found herself trapped inside a dark crevasse. It'd only happened once, but once was enough for her mother.

After checking herself in the mirror and grimacing at what she saw, Avery pulled her beanie back over her unruly brows and climbed down to the first floor. Pumpkin yipped when she saw her new attire, and Oreo, still finishing his meal, wiggled his butt at the opportunity for a hike.

"Where're you going?" her father asked.

"Hiking. I'll be back before it gets dark."

Her mother closed one of her laptops. "You just got home. Where're you going?"

"Just my usual path. I'm taking the dogs, too, if that's okay."

Her mother went for her cane to stand up. "Do you have—?"

Avery dangled her walkie-talkie from the strap.

Her mother sat back down. She pulled her pocketbook to her lap and made sure that she, too, had her walkie-talkie at the ready. She set it beside her phone buzzing with work emails.

"Have fun," her father said, "and watch out for ticks. Check yourself if you walk into any tall grass."

"No tall grass at *all*," her mother added. "You're immediately taking a shower when you come home."

Avery almost shut the door on Oreo's tail. "Got it," she said to the closing door.

As she maneuvered around the patio furniture, Avery finally, *finally* escaped into the forest. Pavement morphed into earth. Fallen leaves became her path. Gone was the normal hike up the hill from school. Now the scent of freedom welcomed her to her second home.

She'd lived her whole life here, in upstate New York. Back in the early nineties, her parents had moved here from Manhattan to be closer to her grandparents. This was back when Avery was still in her mother's belly and her mother didn't need a cane to walk. As her parents worked odd hours, taking business calls outside on the balconies, Avery had spent her time climbing boulders and creating her own trails to lose herself on.

Who needed friends when the Earth welcomed everyone into it? They—the woods, the caves—didn't care about how you looked, they cared if you left only footprints. They didn't make fun of you for wearing the same top more than once. They didn't question the type of person you'd become. They weren't jerks.

Twenty minutes into her hike and Avery's feelings about school and Bridget faded. She'd live easy like this, free of friends who didn't care about your feelings when they knew darn well how much they meant to you. She already had two of the best friends she could ask for, and they didn't even have fleas. *That's* how you treated a real friend.

She came to her favorite parts of the mountain range: the caves. Some of the cooler, deeper caves had tourist traps bitten into them and cost money to experience, but these smaller caves were abandoned to nature. They didn't have fancy waterfalls or crystals in them, and they didn't have railings to keep you from falling, but she didn't mind; she'd gotten trapped between two large rocks when she was twelve, not thirteen. Not that the one-year difference meant a lot, but she had a lot of time to practice spelunking now that her only friend had decided that her company was no longer worth it.

Something magical emanated from these caves, especially when a sudden rain caught her by surprise. She'd hunker down in their entrances, watch the ground darken as water pattered off the ancient rocks. Once, she'd even fallen asleep here, waking up in a panic that she'd been swallowed by something bigger than herself.

As Avery lowered her head to walk in, Oreo turned his black ears to the end of the ominous cave.

"You've been here before," she reminded them. "It's okay."

The couple refused. Oreo planted his butt at the entrance while Pumpkin started licking the walls.

"Hey!" She pulled her back and sat her beside Oreo. "Stay, then. Just know you'll have a lot more fun in there than out here."

Not understanding a word of English, her dogs settled down and waited for her return.

She never found a justification for her fascination with caves, with spelunking, but she guessed most people didn't. They simply crawled into the tight spaces just to say they'd done it. The shivery echoes announced your presence to no one, yet you always felt like you were invading someone's home, stepping into territory you were never prepared for.

Sitting down on a dry spot, she rolled her head back and forth on the cave's grimy wall. She checked the insides of her socks and boots for any ticks, then took off her beanie to ruffle out her long, black hair for twigs. After picking out a few, she studied the pins fixed to her beanie: the one she and Bridget bought at a maple syrup festival, the one marking their survival from their first comic book convention. She rubbed over their nicks and scratch marks. She'd traded both of them with Bridget because she'd wanted the shiny ones.

Avery forced her hat back over her eyes, stretching it down to her chin so she couldn't see. She didn't need her. She'd find a new best friend in a new class. Who cared if she was in almost every class of Avery's? She didn't care for Avery anymore, so neither would she.

Her stomach growled. Moaning, she pulled off her backpack and went for her stash of sour gummy worms.

The rock she was sitting against, once stable and firm, suddenly gave out from behind her, dropping her like a phantom step. This drop, however, didn't have a decorated railing for her to grab on to.

She reached for the wall only to break off a piece in her hand. She kicked out her long legs to catch something, but the ground crumbled beneath her, her backpack her anchor, and she plummeted backwards into darkness.

She tumbled down an invisible decline. Her backpack ripped away from her as stalagmites knocked the wind out of her, making themselves seen. The earth felt colder here, damper with more of a mildew smell than a cave one. She didn't know a cave existed here. She didn't think anything existed beyond these walls.

When the world stopped turning and she heard herself breathe again, she choked on a cry. The soreness rushed her in waves, reminding her of every nerve and muscle she owned. When she found the strength to open her watering eyes, she saw nothing but absolute blackness.

Fearing she'd gone blind from hitting her head, she flipped open her phone.

It didn't help. The space she'd fallen into was so cramped that the walls touched. She couldn't stretch out her legs. She couldn't breathe. She looked up to see where she'd fallen from and saw no light.

Panic swirled in her gut. She couldn't die here. Even if she somehow survived this, her parents would never let her out of the house again. She'd get homeschooled, rumors would spread, Bridget would call her names again...

She shined her phone up the incline. She spotted her backpack hanging on a log. As she angled her light, she discovered a long ladder of prehistoric logs embedded into the wall. Bugs hopped from step to step. In her peripheral vision, they appeared to glow.

Behind her, someone asked a question.

Avery yelped and shined her phone on them like a weapon.

The person yelped back and shielded their eyes. They looked like a boy about her age, but smaller, incredibly small. He carried a handmade backpack with him with a lantern hooked to it—a traveler. His clothes, poked with moth holes, were stitched together with thick stitches like he'd sewn them himself. On his paper-thin, paper-colored skin, Avery saw grooves etched into his inner right forearm. It looked like a map carved from skin.

When she lowered her phone, the boy squinted at her. His left eye was injured due to a thick scar that cut across his face into his nose and cheek. Dirt and other less noticeable scars marred the rest of his skin. He looked in rougher shape than Avery felt.

"I-I need help," she told him. "I fell. I'm hurt. I don't know where I am."

The boy responded back with his own question in his own language. Everything about him, from his words to his strange clothes, seemed otherworldly. When he didn't get the answer he wanted, he balanced on his knees and sniffed her. Whatever he got from her scent, he shook his head and waited to hear an explanation from her that he'd never understand.

Chapter 2: The Autrean

Cameron sat stunned in the Main Exit *Tunnle*. They should've never come here. They'd tried to read their fortune before they left, but their *gemmes* hadn't warned them that they'd run into trouble, much less an Autrean.

Said Autrean continued staring at them, shining that frightful light in their face. She'd finally placed it down like Cameron had been begging her to do, but the light bouncing off the rocks still hurt. It felt like a thousand firebug lanterns lit at once. They thought bringing one lantern with them was enough, but this was blinding. And if they went blind, what good would they be to the Community?

They tried to ask again, "Can you stand? Can you move?" but like they guessed, she didn't understand. Very few Autrean words mirrored Arkeh:nen ones, and it wasn't like they could just bring her back to the surface. Their job since childhood was and would forever be an excavator, a simple folk who gathered *gemmes* for the psychics to use in their practices. They weren't a scavenger. They weren't allowed outside.

The girl asked something. Cameron shook their head, totally lost. Finally gaining back their sight, they found her to be in worse shape than they thought. Her knees were scraped and her palms, a little lighter than her skin, were bleeding.

So dark, this girl. They knew Autreans as dark, like Basil, but this girl had skin and hair as black as a cave.

With simple gestures and smiles, Cameron brought her to her feet. She was definitely the tallest person they'd ever met, but they knew Autreans grew like trees on the surface. Something to do with all that sunlight.

When they turned to go home, the girl didn't follow. Being patient, they took her hand and led her through the *tunnle* somewhat blind.

Not that they needed sight to see. They could've easily found their way home blindfolded. They spent hours in these *tunnles* at a time. The *kaart* etched into their forearm had become obsolete as a navigation map. Now they only looked at it whenever they were excavating a new *tunnle*. Then they'd take a knife and scar a new line down their arm.

The Autrean, however, had difficulties. She'd hurt her leg and needed to palm the *tunnle* walls for guidance. Cameron warned her about incoming stalactites, but she somehow hit each and every one.

The *tunnle* ended with a beautifully decorated blanket stitched by a beautifully aged Grandmoeder. It draped over the entrance hole and welcomed back scavengers who braved the outside world. Symbols of nature and rocks were sewn into the precious fabric, illustrating their history of digging back into the Earth.

Cameron carefully parted the blanket to reveal their world of Arkeh:na.

Since they left, more of the *ville shoppes* had opened up for the day. The owners of each little shack dusted off their quilts and trinkets they'd trade for squirrel meat or *gemmes*. Cameron had woken up earlier than usual to avoid being hounded down by *shoppekeeps* for being where they weren't supposed to be. They just had an inkling to come to the Main Exit *Tunnle*, and now, evidently, they knew why. They just wished their *gemmes* had better prepared them. They would've brought some healing ointments with them.

Behind the *ville* shacks were the stairs and ladders leading down into the layers of Arkeh:na. Cutting through it flowed the *Rivière*, the winding river that split the *ville* in half, and the *Centrum*, the main pavilion where people lounged about and gossiped.

To the right of the *Rivière* was the washing pond and its waterfalls, the psychics' underground reading dens, and the artisan huts. There, seamstresses, pottery makers, and cooks prepared for the day. A few early birds had started the day right, calling out orders from inside the sweaty mud huts and sewing up new outfits for their friends and family. As Cameron trotted over the tiny bridge across the *Rivière*, they saw neither Basil nor Maywood anywhere. Strange. Maywood usually stayed close to Basil to keep him from running away from his duties.

They lost the girl's hand. She fell back on the bridge, her jaw slowly dropping. She took in the height of the *Centrum's* pillars and the noise from the artisan huts. The more she experienced, the wider her mouth opened.

When she started rubbing her arms up and down in shock, Cameron took back her limp hand and led her to the seamstress' huts. They avoided looking down at the ladder leading to the psychics' dens. The energy from down there radiated through the bridge into their moccasins.

They never spent too much time on this side of the *Rivière*. Their lack of technical skills had no place with so many talented people. Cameron had been gifted with the rare sense to locate and extract *gemmes* in the caves, but nobody cared, and they understood that. Their *Moeder* was the most powerful psychic in the Community. Everyone came to her when their lives became too heavy to bear alone. When Cameron had been born, everyone was ready to welcome another equally talented psychic to the family.

Instead, Cameron had become a jinx, one who caused frequent cave-ins and zapped the energy from every *gemme* they touched. They tried to make up for this by hunting down the best *gemmes*, but all they came back with were dead rocks and lost Autreans.

Seamstresses were working hard inside the mud huts. Their silkworms buzzed as balls of thread were fished from their cages.

Maywood, sitting at her usual spinning wheel, looked up to greet Cameron. Then she noticed the Autrean girl and took her foot off the pedal.

"It's okay," Cameron said. Before she sat up and used most of her strength for the day, they leaned down and held her hands. She was Basil's older sister, the more dependable one of the family. "I found her at the Main Exit. I think she fell, but I can't understand her."

The Autrean girl said something in an exasperated tone. She started wandering around the kilns and the pottery left out to dry. She went to touch an unfinished bowl, then thought better of herself and pulled back to admire the craft without touching it.

"You shouldn't have brought her down here," Maywood warned. "They're not allowed here. You know that."

"I know, but she's hurt. I was wondering if you could mend her clothes. Then I was going to bring her to a healer."

A few artisans pulled back from their work and whispered about the newcomer. Cameron's Moeder had often told them not to worry about how people thought of them, but that was impossible. They wanted to do good by everyone, Arkeh:nen and Autrean alike, but what could they say to the adults? That they were wrong for being distrustful of Autreans? Most kids Cameron's age were intrigued by Autreans and wanted to learn more about them, but they knew the older generations had their reservations. Their ancestors had buried themselves away for a reason.

Maywood scratched her thinning hairline. "When's the last time an Autrean came here? I can't remember."

Cameron shrugged. They'd never seen one personally, but they heard the rumors. They rode on loud machines called "cars," took up more space than they could fit in. They were so close to being Arkeh:nen, but that thick layer of sediment made enough of a difference to them.

"This's serious, isn't it?" Maywood asked. "Should we tell the Grandmoeders about this?"

"No," Cameron said promptly. "I can't worry them with something like this. She just needs help, then we can send her on her way. Are there any healers awake yet?"

As Maywood went to answer, someone slammed into the doorless archway of the mud hut.

Basil snapped upright. Balls of silk clung to his bearskin dress. It looked like he'd tried to transfer the cocoons to the boilers for processing, but had accidentally fallen into one of the nests.

He ripped off the sticky cocoons as he gawked at the Autrean. "Who the heck is this?"

It sounded like he asked the same question to the Autrean in her native tongue. He knew how to speak basic Autrean from his time as a scavenger, but the girl still didn't answer.

"I brought her," Cameron told him.

"Why? Cameron, you know they're dangerous. Were you at the exit *tunnles* again?"

"Lower your voice," Maywood hushed. "It's too early to argue."

"I found her at the Main Exit," Cameron explained. "She's hurt."

"The Main—That's the closest one to the Autreans! She needs to go back. I'm taking her back."

"She's hurt," they insisted. "We have to help her."

"She's *Autrean*."

"And we're *Arkeh:nen*, and Arkeh:nen help anyone who needs it."

Basil bit his cheek, battling a truth they'd been taught since birth. Ever since the early times, Arkeh:nen had a duty to protect those seeking help. Whether you were running from bears or hateful talk, a cave was a place to hide from your worries until you felt safe enough to leave.

The girl backed away. She kept shaking her head and repeating a phrase over and over again. Then, from the build-up of her fall, from Arkeh:na, and from not being acknowledged, she screamed. She hollered and let out everything trapped inside of her. She pointed at Cameron, then at Maywood, then took it upon herself to explore

Arkeh:na alone. Tripping over a spinning wheel, she pushed past Basil and disappeared.

Chapter 3: The Lake

She must've fallen into an elaborate medieval reenactment. Somewhere in this open cave she'd find ball gowns and knights clashing swords. She needed to. It was the only explanation for such a place existing.

With her leg twinging in pain, she escaped the mud hut and ran for the tunnel where she'd fallen from.

Four miners blocked her path. They had types of cigarettes in their mouths and were covered in dirt. They wore mining helmets and lanterns attached to their belts. When Avery tried to pass them, they whispered secrets about her behind their hands.

She scrambled backwards and ran down the length of the river. She just needed to follow its current to find her way home. When the boy had led her down that tunnel, she'd tried to call her parents to save her, but the calls hadn't gone through, and her walkie was somewhere in her bag. Down here, she had no contact with the outside world.

In the shantytown of shacks, shopkeeps came out and asked her questions she couldn't understand. One even grabbed her arm and pointed to her knee. The aroma of spices along with the cacophony of metal noises made her shriek, "I don't know!" and barrel through the crowd.

There must've been another person here who spoke English, right? That boy covered in bugs spoke it. *"Why the hell you here?"* She hoped to never see him again. He sounded like Bridget and every other bully who hated her for no reason.

She followed the cave's natural curves down a wide staircase. She couldn't stop her feet. Lanterns and torches were lit down here, but they didn't do much. It must've been enough for this society.

Hidden within these dark levels grew an entire village of people. The floors spiraled down into a dark pit. Creaky bridges and ladders connected everything together. People were hanging their laundry out to dry over the abysses, where children dangled from railings and called out to their friends below.

And these people, who were chatting with their neighbors and living peacefully, they were bandaged like that girl upstairs—Mayard, Maywood? Most of them were scarred and using canes like her mother. What was this place? A homeless camp? A prison?

She slid down a rotting ladder and continued running. She passed by mothers toting around children and men hauling buckets of water on their heads. Sometimes she passed a curtained hole in the wall, but when she darted through it, she was in somebody's home. They were cramped caves decorated with tapestry and gemstones. Each cave person looked more surprised to see her than the next.

Running out of places to hide, Avery jumped through a doorless doorway and froze. Nobody had lit a lantern this way. She reached out in front of her: left or right, each way just as dark.

"Hey!"

The two boys from before had caught up with her. They darted around other cave people in order to grab her. What had she done wrong? It hadn't been her choice to come down here. Was she in trouble?

She sucked in the musty air and chose to go right. While she sensed that the scarred boy was nice, she couldn't tell with the other one, and she didn't want to ask what she'd done to make him so angry.

As the boys' yelling faded, a pinpoint of light came into focus.

A moss-covered door blocked her way. Etched into the wood were drawings of elegant women cloaked in blankets. Two lanterns lit each side, but they were lit by rocks, not bugs. Some type of blue gem emitted a cool light within the glass.

Avery checked around it. Like she guessed, no outlets, no power cords. This society somehow thrived on nothing but dirt and glowing rocks.

"Stop!"

The two boys had found her. The scarred boy wheezed and coughed from running so hard, the angry one looked ready to fight.

"Don't go in there!" he warned in English. "Not allowed!"

Ignoring him, Avery wrestled with the wooden door and thrust it open.

The scarred boy fell back on his butt and shielded his eyes with both arms. The angry boy cursed and turned away just as Avery shut the door behind her.

It felt like she locked herself in a meat freezer. As the heavy door slammed shut, she checked if she could see her breath.

Gemstones as tall as people glowed around the room. In puddles, in the stream cutting through the floor, some even held up the ceiling as support beams. There were no lanterns here, not even a skylight for the Sun to peek through. Just crystallized magic, and a group of cloaked people.

Six elderly women gawked at her from the wall. They sat comfortably in furs and blankets and wore shawls decorated with animal bones and gem fragments. A few young children took care of them, but something more than the presence of a crowd froze Avery to the ground.

The serene, sickly-looking grandmothers carried more power in their eyes than her principal when he patrolled the halls. They glared at her without speaking, but she somehow knew how each of them felt about her. Catching her breath, she stepped back from what felt like disturbed Goddesses.

A grandmother with bright blue eyes smiled at her. "Finally, she came down."

Another grandmother pointed a judgmental finger at Avery. "Who gave you permission to enter? Why're you here?"

The power these women had slammed Avery against the wall. She couldn't stand it when adults got upset with her, but a grandparent's anger equated to getting whacked across the cheek.

Avery stuttered, "I-I'm sorry!" and flew through the room. She kept her head down out of respect and out of shame. Hopping over the blue stream, she ran for the only other door in the room and pushed it open.

She began panting. She didn't know where else to go. Ever since she'd fallen down here, she hadn't found any stairs leading up. Just down, down, deeper into the Earth's core.

Her boots sunk into wet sand. She'd come across a pond, a slate of grey that stretched out like a baseball field. Waterfalls sparkled down the rocks as droplets of water dripped off the ceiling. Not a lot of vegetation grew here, but with the help of three skylights a hundred feet above, grass and lilies had formed in the pond. Fish swam in place as they stared at Avery through the weeds.

The misty air cooled her down and splashed her face with clarity. She needed to calm down before she broke down. If she fell apart here, she'd never get home.

She spotted a small hill overlooking the pond and struggled her way to it. Her boots, while designed for hiking, had trouble gripping the dunes. When she reached the top, she took out her phone and searched for a signal.

Her call didn't even last a ring. Even this close to the surface, her parents were still too far away.

She dropped to her knees. They'd been right. They had every right to worry. She thought she was so much stronger than this, but now she felt more lost than ever. She'd lost her walkie, lost her way. She'd lost her mind, clearly, being that she was underground talking to cave dwellers.

Quiet sniffling burned her eyes. She wanted to go home. At least there she could cry in her bathroom and her parents knew not to call her down for dinner until the bathroom fan turned off.

As she cleaned her face on her sweater, wet footsteps echoed across the pond.

She startled. The boy with the scarred face was at the pond, holding onto a crystallized rock as he coughed.

Avery hid her eyes with her beanie. She knew she ugly-cried. Nobody, especially a boy her age, needed to see the worst side of her.

The boy climbed up to her cliff.

"I'm sorry," she said. "I'm okay, I swear."

The boy sat beside her. He stared out across the pond, taking in the stillness of the water. This was probably the only place in this world where you could sit down and hear yourself breathe, or wheeze in his case.

He took something out of his poncho. Hidden underneath was a necklace entangled with gems. Its cord was made of rope or twine and looked strong enough to withstand the weight of each gem. The gems themselves varied in color, but most of them shared the same hue of aqua blue, her favorite color.

After inspecting one of the stones, the boy sat up and placed the necklace around her neck.

She raised the largest gem to her eye. Each one was twisted in pointed metal. If they hit the light right, they reflected a rainbow. "Pretty."

The boy said something back.

"What language are you speaking?"

He pursed his lips and waited for a better explanation.

She asked, "Do you have a name?"

"Name—*Naam*?" he clarified. "Cameron."

"Cameron?" She'd heard the boy in the mud hut say that, but she hadn't been sure. "I'm Avery. Avery Marlow."

"Avery?" He poked her arm. "Avery!"

"Yeah."

"*Ja!*"

"Jah?" She giggled, though it hurt too much. She cradled her injured side.

Cameron lost his playful smile and touched her leg, making her jump. Then he said something to her and took her hand.

"Where're we going?" she asked, and she wasn't sure, but under his breath, she thought she heard him say, "My mother."

Chapter 4: Moeder Ellinor

Cameron tried their hardest not to cough in front of the girl. The chase had left them exhausted. To keep her from noticing and to stop her from crying, they'd given her one of their necklaces to wear. Parting from personal *gemmes* always stung, but they'd worked their wonderful magic yet again. She'd stop crying. She was smiling.

Sitting up slowly so their vision didn't blot out, Cameron took Avery's hand and led her away from the Lake. They'd never entered the Lake den without first being given an errand to run. They weren't a water cleanser or toilet cleaner. They knew their way around sure enough, but they couldn't help but trace the lines making up their *kaart*, wondering when they'd walk this path again.

Avery pointed to the scars.

"My *kaart*," they explained. They wanted to go on in detail about this important part of themselves—literally—but they held back. She wouldn't understand. The *kaart* was carved into each Arkeh:nen's arm at thirteen so they never got lost. Families would celebrate the milestone with fresh meat and new candles. After a disastrous cave-in at twelve years old, Cameron had earned theirs a year earlier than most. Not many neighbors celebrated it, however they, Basil, Maywood, and their Moeder shared a squirrel together.

Not knowing how to explain that to her, Cameron just said, "It helps us get around so we don't get lost."

"Oh."

They left the Lake quickly. This, they wouldn't get in trouble for, but the *Grandmoeders'* Den? A shiver crawled up their neck. Avery, an *outsider*, had barged into their Den without permission. Seeing them unannounced like that would brandish you with shame for the rest of your life. Hopefully the Grandmoeders would be lenient with her misdoing. If they weren't, they'd gladly take the punishment for her. It was their fault, after all.

Like they thought, a crowd had begun to form around the *tunnle* entrance. The Community held up firebug lanterns and glowing *gemmes* to get a better look at the newcomer. Whenever someone got too close, Avery ducked away.

"She's scared," Cameron told them. "Please don't do that."

"Where'd you find her?"

"Did you bring her down yourself?"

"Do the Grandmoeders know?"

"Did a psychic predict this?"

Not wanting to stir up any rumors, Cameron nudged themselves out of the crowd and headed home. Multiple pairs of eyes lingered on them from the higher levels. They made haste and slipped down the ladders.

One woman trotted over not with questions but with a jar of her famous honey wrapped in a blade of river grass. Her name was Claire. She used to be Cameron's teacher before they graduated to become an excavator.

"Here," she said, handing it to Cameron. "My lover collected this yesterday and had it purified by the psychics. It should help calm things down."

"Are you sure?" Cameron asked, noting how heavy the bottle felt.

"Yes, but be quick." She eyed the upper levels. Two children hid themselves. "The energy's tense here. People are whispering. Best to use this in a secluded spot and drink it slow and meaningfully."

"I will. Thank you."

She gave an acknowledging nod to Avery before running her hand through Cameron's poofy hair. "Take care, dear. This might be challenging for you, but you can overcome it."

"Thank you," they said, and ran down the nearest rock staircase. The steep steps took Avery by surprise—she grabbed hold of their shoulders to keep from falling—but Cameron supported her and escaped to the lowest level of Arkeh:na.

The dens down here had been built less than thirty years ago by their brave ancestors. They were by far the newest additions to Arkeh:na, but Cameron knew their ancestors had wanted to dig even deeper.

Cameron was a sixth generation Arkeh:nen and prided themselves on keeping up their heritage. Everything their ancestors had given up weighed down on their every move. This meant taking care of everyone who needed help.

They loved their Community. They loved it so much that, when they were taught their history, they discovered a pronoun some people went by: "they." At first, they thought this meant the person's actions were tied to the

Community. "They" were "the Community." Intrigued, they researched into it, then found out what it really meant. It was for a person who didn't feel like a "boy" or "girl." It separated them from the pretty girls in their class and the rowdy boys who played in the mud. It gave them an option they never knew was there.

That week, they proudly announced to their class to call them a "they" instead of their old pronoun.

Each den had decorative drapery acting as their door. Some had animal pelts, sewn-together furs of squirrels and rabbits. Some, like Cameron's den, had an antique blanket a Grandmoeder had sewn for them. Whenever Cameron passed by their door, they rubbed the soft, ancient fabric, feeling the energy their own birth Grandmoeder had put into it.

They basically had their den to themselves. Their Fader had disappeared when they were six and their Moeder barely left the psychics' dens. With the extra room, they'd filled their 100-square-foot space with curios: torn pieces of fabric from their old baby clothes; drying lavender tied to the walls; pieces of glass that almost looked like *gemmes*.

None of them compared to their actual collection of *gemmes*, gemstones they'd personally dug out from the Earth. They were kept in special boxes or, if they were tall enough, stood upright against the walls. Over the course of their life, Cameron had excavated around 2,000 *gemmes*, but had only kept around 200. The rest became gifts for the Community.

They escorted Avery inside of their bed, a long hole cut into the floor. With her size, she could've easily rested her chin on the edge, but she didn't. She instead pulled herself into a ball and sat quietly in the corner next to their *gemme* shelves.

Cameron smirked at her. So tall, yet so conscious of her space.

They offered her the jar of honey. "You can eat this to calm down." They pretended to drink down the bottle. "*Eat.* It's good."

"*Eaten?*" She tipped back her head to taste it.

She dropped the bottle and pointed above her in horror.

Cameron's bat, Nuvu, was hanging upside down on her metal mesh. When Basil was still a scavenger, he'd scavenged the piece from a junkyard and hammered it into the wall for them. She'd made her nest in the corner, and claimed Cameron's whole den as hers.

"That's my bat," Cameron explained. "Nuvu."

"*Nuvu?*"

"Yeah. She kind of hates people. I'm not even sure she likes me." They climbed into bed with her. Their bear pelt kept them from skinning their knees. "Do Autreans know what bats are? Have you ever seen one? They only live in caves and only like Arkeh:nen."

Avery shrugged and lapped the hardened honey circling the top of the jar. It reminded Cameron of how Nuvu ate honey, but with her reddened eyes and scratched face, she looked less likely to bite one of Cameron's fingers.

She caught their eyes and asked them a question.

"I want to learn more about you," they blurted out. "We're not allowed to talk to Autreans if we ever see one in the wild, but I've never seen one before. Well, Basil's half-Autrean, but he was born and raised here."

Avery pulled something out of her pocket. Before Cameron could ask, that bright light blinded them yet again.

"Sorry!" She lowered the brightness, but Cameron still needed to squint to see. Basil always told them stories about these devices. Autreans called them "fones."

Avery tapped something on her *fone* and showed it to them.

Even though it hurt, Cameron moved up closer to see the moving picture. It was of a blue and green orb surrounded by blackness. White clouds stretched around it as it spun like a ball.

"*Cool,*" they awed. "What is it?"

She clicked her *fone* and a new picture popped up, one of green trees and mossy logs: her world. The Autre world.

Biting their lower lip, Cameron took the *fone* and scrolled for themselves. They weren't allowed to enter the Autre world, but could they see pictures of it? They hoped so, because they'd never, ever felt so much intrigue by something outside of Arkeh:na. The endless rivers not cut off by rock, the flowers growing with help from the Sun. How far did the sky stretch? How tall did the trees grow? Arkeh:na had its tight-knit charm, but this was world-altering.

As they frantically searched for more pictures, Cameron stumbled across a picture not blessed by earthly qualities, but by graphite.

They had an understanding of the Autrean written word. Having neither the tree supply nor light for it, Arkeh:nen hardly ever wrote, but from time to time, scavengers would sneak back papers for the Community to see. They always gathered a crowd whenever a picture book came down.

But in these photos, it seemed like someone had taken pictures *of* drawings. The sketchy people had been drawn with exaggerated features, particularly in the eyes and hair. They all looked sad for some reason, but also beautiful.

Avery yanked back her *fone* and hid away the pictures.

"Did you draw those?" Cameron asked. "Avery, you?"

"Yes, me." She filtered through the pictures more quickly, as if too shy to show off her own work.

"Can you teach me how to draw?" they insisted. "Can you draw me? No Arkeh:nen is good at drawing, and these are really good."

Avery beamed red. She blushed so easily that Cameron couldn't stop themselves from feeding her more praise.

Someone pushed back their doorway blanket.

Maywood peeked her head in and greeted them with a smile and friendly wave. Basil, arms crossed, stood beside her.

"Hello there," Maywood said to Avery. "It's nice to see you again. My, she probably doesn't understand a word I'm saying, does she?"

"I don't think so," Cameron said.

"I told you," Basil said. "No Autrean understands our language. Only the Grandmoeders know their words. And why is she in your bed? Get her out of there."

"No. She's still hurt."

"So bring her to a psychic. Find a healer. Your neighbor's good at healing, isn't she?"

Cameron fiddled with a gemstone on their necklace. In truth, they were acquainting Avery to their world. In actuality, they were scared. Terrified. Keeping her here made her happy, but also kept them in the clear. Once their Moeder found out...

Maywood squatted beside Cameron's bed and balanced her cane on her lap. "My name is Maywood. *May-wood*. I work with the silkworms. And this's my brother, Basil. We're good friends of Cameron."

Basil curled his upper lip in a pout. "She won't understand."

"Maywood." Avery pointed to said girl, then to Basil. "Basil?"

Basil's nostrils flared. "Well, that's easy. They're names. Her accent's still off."

"I've heard your Autrean isn't that good, either," Maywood said with a sneer, "yet you still practice it in our den. She'll learn it in time."

"No, she won't. She's not staying. She has to leave."

"You're right."

That voice, so deep and willful, seeded Cameron back into reality. They hardly heard it anymore, but that steady tone would've brought anyone fooling around back to attention.

Cameron's Moeder, one of the most paramount psychics in all of Arkeh:na, stood in the doorway with her hands on her hips, glaring down at Cameron and Avery.

"I knew I shouldn't have left you alone this morning," she said. "Bring her here, then. I'll deal with her myself."

Chapter 5: The Grandmoeders' Call

Whatever mood Avery had created with Cameron and his friends died when the woman walked in. She looked like a mom, so nothing like her own mother: wide hips, shoulder-length hair, and a somewhat wrinkled face. She wore a poncho similar to Cameron's, but around her waist like a skirt, and she wore more gemstones than he did. The rings on her fingers looked like they cost a grand each.

With a wave of her hand, both Basil and Maywood jumped out of the way and stood alert at the edge of the room. Cameron scampered out of his bed/hole to give her a place to sit. She took it graciously and sat in front of Avery, and a sense of drowning filled up the hole. Not even Avery's own mother commanded so much from her, with those stern eyes and unblinking stare. If this woman told her to run out of this hole and never come back, she'd be trekking through the forest before she finished her demand.

Cameron and Basil squatted at the edge of the bed like gargoyles, waiting for the woman to speak. Maywood took worried glances out of the room to see if she could escape without being noticed.

The woman spoke. Once she finished, Basil said in English, "Uh, this is...mother of Cameron, Moeder Ellinor. She is great psychic. She will help."

"Are you translating for her?" Avery asked.

"I have to. I shouldn't, although. You cannot be here."

Moeder Ellinor reached out for Avery's arm and pushed up her sweater to examine the bruises. While she spoke, she took out an old container of paste and spread it over the wounds. Avery couldn't tell her to stop, mostly because she trusted this "Moeder's" actions.

Her skin prickled like a thousand ants were crawling up her arm. She shrieked in alarm, but Cameron's mother kept a firm hand on her wrist, keeping her still.

"It always feels weird," Basil interpreted. "Mushroom medicine, it's fine."

"But mushrooms are poisonous."

Basil smirked. "You think we know not about mushrooms? We're more smarter than you Autreans act."

Cameron asked his Moeder a question in a mousy voice.

She shook her head, then checked Avery's forehead temperature with her hand. She too had an intricate scar on her forearm, although hers was more faded than everyone else's.

"She...wants you to see that...you're mysterious," Basil explained, then muttered something under his breath that made Cameron hit him. He continued, "However...you are welcome here, in Arkeh:na."

"*Ar-kay-nah?*"

"This, our home, us people. You should...not stay long, although. Most—*All*— Arkeh:nen hate Autreans, you people from the surface. We help...everyone, although we shouldn't."

Moeder Ellinor said something that made Basil cover his mouth in politeness. Then she spoke to Avery.

"She asks if you hurt in more places," Basil said through his fingers.

"No," Avery lied, "but thank you for helping me."

Moeder Ellinor rubbed the top of Avery's hand, addressed something to Cameron, and began to stand.

A soft chime dinged throughout the room. It came from a golden bell attached above the curtained entrance. The string connected to it was being yanked by someone impatient.

All four cave people bolted upright and stared at the bell until it stopped. They waited as if to hear dire news from a primitive air raid siren.

"*Crap*," Basil whispered.

Moeder Ellinor jumped out of the hole and jogged out of the den.

Cameron, shaken, helped Avery up. Maywood asked a flurry of questions. Basil kept cursing as he paced across the room.

"What does the bell mean?" Avery asked.

"The Grandmoeders call us," Basil said. "This is trouble. We shouldn't be doing this. Bad—" He complained more to Maywood in their language.

Cameron ignored him. He kept massaging Avery's hand, assuring her that everything would be alright. It didn't calm her down.

She tried her best to keep up with Cameron's Moeder. Cameron took small, nervous steps down the ladders and through the halls. Maywood had her cane. Basil stayed behind them with his head down.

Families peeked out of their homes to watch them go. With more time to take in this world, Avery saw multiple lengths of string secured to the top of the ceiling. The only one moving was the one connected to Cameron's house. The rest were dutifully quiet.

She tried to hide her face underneath her beanie, but Cameron took her hand. Following his Moeder, they entered into the tunnel she'd accidentally run into, the one leading to the "Grandmoeders."

An attendant who'd been catering to the elderly women hid behind the moss-covered door. They whispered secrets to Moeder Ellinor, then glared at Avery as they brightened their lantern. Then they cracked open the door and escorted them inside.

The eldest Grandmoeder, the one who'd first talked to Avery when she'd stormed in, raised her bony hand. "Come in."

Cameron helped push Avery in. Her feet stuck to the floor, begging her to run back. She'd caused such a scene a half-hour ago. What could she say to them now?

When she, Cameron, and Cameron's Moeder walked in, the attendant shut the door on Maywood and Basil. They didn't argue, but they did cast apprehensive looks through the closing space. Before the door shut, Basil shouted a warning to Cameron.

"Why can't they come in with us?" Avery whispered.

Cameron didn't say. His eyes were spellbound on the smiling grandmother.

Somehow, entering the Grandmoeders' Den with purpose made Avery more nervous. Now all of them were sitting up in their beds of furs. One of them needed the wall to rest on. Bandages covered her face like a mummy. She looked asleep, or dead.

Cameron and his mother knelt before the Grandmoeders, Moeder Ellinor with grace, Cameron with some difficulty. His knees kept cracking.

Avery copied them with little instruction. The stream in the room encircled them like a prison cell and kept them from moving around too much.

"Raise your heads."

The Grandmoeder spoke in Cameron's language, but it sounded similar to English, enough for Avery to follow.

The kind Grandmoeder smiled down at them. The others cast down scowls. The one who'd yelled at Avery to get out had a bulging vein in her forehead.

"Welcome to our home," the nice Grandmoeder said in English. "My name is Grandmoeder Geneva. I see you've met my daughter Ellinor and her child Cameron."

At hearing their names, the two family members bowed their heads. Cameron's head hit the ground with honor.

"Yes," Avery said. "Thank you for taking me in."

"Company keeps the soul less lonely. As you might've guessed by our reactions, we don't see many surface people come through our doors. Let me ask you this: How did you happen across our settlement?"

"I tripped. I was resting my back against the wall and it caved in. That's when Cameron found me. He helped me."

The Grandmoeder next to Grandmoeder Geneva grumbled something.

"Grandmoeder Nai wishes to address," said Grandmoeder Geneva, "that the pronoun you use for my grandchild is wrong."

"Huh?"

"Cameron Quinn is neither a girl nor a boy, neither man nor woman. They have chosen to call themselves by the Community's pronoun of 'they'. Be sure to keep that in mind when addressing them from now on."

Avery, baffled, looked to Cameron, who must've heard his name and was now waiting for a translation.

She'd never known anyone to go by anything other than the pronoun they looked like. He looked like a boy. He sounded like a boy.

Delayed embarrassment welled up inside of her. Why was this part of life so difficult to get right? Why did people put so much emphasis on the most embarrassing part of themselves? He—they?—didn't seem embarrassed by it, so why was she?

"Anywho," Grandmoeder Geneva continued, "we're happy you're here. Interaction between us and Autreans is limited, so any new encounter is recognized."

"But it's not welcomed," Grandmoeder Nai said.

"But it can be," another chimed in.

"But should it?" asked another.

Avery closed her eyes from dizziness. What could she say that they'd understand? Should she talk about Cameron's kindness and save them from being reprimanded? Should she apologize for being alive? Should she run?

"Do you have any questions for us, child?" Grandmoeder Geneva asked.

Avery licked her lips. "I...think I'd like to know how you all got here. How long have you been living here?"

"We've been here for generations, ever since the pilgrims voyaged across the ocean in search of land. Our ancestors hid themselves within the Earth to avoid persecution for one reason or the next. Witches afraid of being burned, families who could no longer afford the land they'd stolen. As time grew, they chose this world instead of the one above, and we keep their spirits alive by keeping underground."

"Do the surface people—us Autreans—know about you?"

"You're the first of your generation to visit us."

"Best to keep this secret to yourself," Grandmoeder Nai said. "You shan't be telling others about us, do you understand?"

"I-I would never. I don't have any friends, so I have no one to tell."

"Is that true?" Grandmoeder Geneva said. "Do you really have no friends?"

"Yeah, and my parents don't care about what I do, so they won't care where I've been."

Grandmoeder Geneva took that in, then beckoned for one of her attendants. They brought her a bag.

"My bag," Avery said.

They took out an object crackling with energy.

"My walkie."

"Such a curious machine," Grandmoeder Geneva said, playing with the antenna. She handed it back to the servant who then rushed it and the backpack to Avery. "However separate you are from your parents, I'm sure they must be waiting for you."

Avery checked her phone. It was nearly seven. "I think you're right."

"But before you leave, I must tell you something: Your presence here has affected our Community in a way we haven't felt in a long time. Some of us"—she nodded to Grandmoeder Nai—"still hold prejudices against Autreans, but I believe you can help us see a light we haven't basked in for several centuries. May I ask, if you wish, that you come by once more?"

Avery lifted her head. "I can come back?"

"If you wish to learn more," she said, then smiled just as widely as Avery did.

"O-okay," she said almost as a question. "I'd love to. This place is incredible. You're all incredible."

"You're very kind," Grandmoeder Geneva said. "Now, I think it's time you leave us. It's getting late for you." She turned to Cameron and Moeder Ellinor and spoke to them in their language, something Avery now wanted to learn more than ever. They both nodded with everything she said, then stood up at the same time when she finished. Cameron's Moeder went to their bedsides so they could whisper more discreetly. Cameron took the lantern from the attendant before taking Avery's hand. He was a very physical person.

They were a very physical person.

Back on the first level of Arkeh:na, the village shops were still buzzing like a beehive. Because of this, instead of cutting through it, Cameron snuck around the shacks back to the tunnel where they first met. She'd noticed that when they'd left the pond, they'd defended her from the crowds, swatting their hands away from her. She needed to learn how to say "thank you" in their language. They were too kind to her.

The boulder she'd dislodged from her fall was now back in place. Now only Cameron's lantern provided them light.

The two of them stood there at the end of the tunnel, waiting for either Avery to start climbing or Cameron to leave.

"I'm sorry if I got you and your mom in trouble," Avery said. "Were those your elders or something, like a counsel? The Grandmoeders?"

"Grandmoeders, yes."

"I wish I knew your language. I could teach you English and you can teach me...Arkeh:nen."

At that special name drop, Cameron smiled.

"Well." She bit her inner cheek. "Bye."

They pointed at her chest, and only when she looked down did she realize they were pointing at her necklace and not something else.

"Oh." She went to give it back, but Cameron let her keep it with hesitant hands. It looked as if they didn't actually want to let it go.

"Are you sure?"

They nodded, but if they understood her, she didn't know.

Neither of them moved. In the dim light, they stood knowing this might've been the last time either of them saw their kind again.

But that wasn't true. She'd promised to return. Her parents would question her extended trips into the woods, but she'd think of an excuse later. Like she'd tell them a word about what she just unearthed.

Her cell phone vibrated in her hands. A slow string of texts were beginning to channel through.

Being the catalyst she needed, Avery gave Cameron one last look before she climbed up the ladder.

Chapter 6: Reality

The darkness had stolen away her dogs as well as the Sun. She'd totally forgotten about them. And the time. Was it still even Friday? Ever since the fall, her thoughts and emotions had gotten scrambled, like she'd been walking through a haze until she resurfaced to the surface world.

She pushed the boulder back into place and took in the empty, strikingly uninteresting cave. The dull smell, the quietness, nothing gave away the society living a mere hundred feet beneath her feet.

A loud barking echoed throughout the cave, and before she could make sure it wasn't a police dog searching for her missing body, Oreo barreled into her. He got so excited that he nipped off her hat.

Avery used her remaining strength to push him off. "Where's Pumpkin? Did she make it home?"

He jumped up and kept nuzzling her. His fur was slick with rain. She knew that he would've stayed with her until he knew she was safe. Pumpkin, while lovably silly, would've run as soon as she smelled trouble.

Her walkie-talkie, once struggling to work, sparked back to life. She fiddled with its buttons for reception. "Mom?"

She waited about three seconds before she heard a crash. "Avery? Avery, is that you?"

"I'm here."

"Where've you *been*?" her mother almost shouted. "I've been trying to get a hold of you for hours! Are you okay? What happened?"

She kicked at the boulder holding back all of Arkeh:na. "I got sidetracked."

"Well, come home! It's supposed to rain any second—I'm watching the weather channel right now. Come home!"

Avery stared at her walkie-talkie as droplets of rain dripped off the cave entrance. After about a minute of processing, she made sure she had everything in her backpack before jogging back home. Oreo trotted faithfully behind her.

She started at a slow pace, but soon found herself running, her fingers wound up in Cameron's necklace. Puddles dared to be jumped in. Fallen trees became hurdles to hop over. A confusing laugh spilled out of her, joyous and light, and kept her from crying over life's uncertainties.

She had the chance, to make a friend, who wouldn't know a thing about her past. They accepted outcasts. They hated the outside world. She was, apart from Basil's thinking, liked and wanted, something she never thought she deserved to be.

She squealed into her hands with glee. Oreo barked with her until the tips of their cabin came into view.

Pumpkin spun in circles as she waited for them inside the garage. Oreo reunited with her in a pounce that tripped up the garage spotlight. If their barking hadn't given her away, the spotlight lighting up the entire driveway sure did.

Her mother and father were in their usual spots: mom at the dinner table, dad in the kitchen. But neither of them were working. They had their phones clutched in their hands as they paced in the dark. When Avery opened the door, her mother slammed down her phone and strode towards her.

"Sorry," Avery said immediately.

"Why was Pumpkin here before you? Where were you? Why didn't you pick up?"

She dared to look down at her phone, but she couldn't break eye contact with her mother. "I...found this pond. It had koi in it. I was wondering who they belonged to, so I went door to door. I was so busy talking to this one woman, I forgot to call in. My walkie was...in my bag."

Her mother checked her torn leggings. "You're hurt."

"I, uh, tried to get a closer look at the koi, but tripped and fell into the water. I think that's why my walkie-talkie wasn't picking up any signals."

"Let me see it," her father said. "I can fix it."

"Why were there koi fish in the forest?" her mother asked. "Who did they belong to?"

"I'm not sure. I think they've lived there all their life."

"Well, koi fish live an awfully long time in the wild," her father noted.

"When have koi fish ever been able to live outside of a tank?" Her mother walked back to her table, back to work now that her daughter had flown back to the nest. "Avery, get washed up and clean out your socks. We'll do your laundry tonight. God, don't ever stay out that late again. You scared us."

"We already ate," her father said. "I sectioned up the leftovers and put them in the fridge. Top one is yours."

The fresh taste of Arkeh:nen honey still lingered on Avery's tongue, but she couldn't go to bed without eating something. After washing her hands of cave dirt, she made herself a plate of cheesy potatoes and lamb. To avoid any more questions about her totally unbelievable story, she ascended up the stairs without a word.

"Hey."

She gripped her plate hard. "Yeah?"

Her father hooked around the stairs. "What's that around your neck?"

"Oh." The Arkeh:nen jewelry felt commonplace in the tunnels, but outside, it did seem to stand out. The gems were uneven, the rope frayed. She hid the largest gem in her fist, the metal digging into her palm. "I made it. I found some stones and rope in the woods."

"Wow. That's impressive. Juniper, did you see this?"

Avery pulled down on the necklace. She couldn't stand their praise, even if it was genuine. One time she'd shown them a drawing of hers that'd taken hours to make. Her mother gave it a once-over, then proceeded to point out all the flaws she saw in it. That's when she stopped drawing downstairs. She couldn't stand their eyes on her heart.

"I saw," her mother said. "Did you wash the stones before you touched them, Avery? I don't want you getting sick from them."

"I did," Avery said, and deflated a bit. Was she expecting praise? She hadn't even made it.

"Well, it's neat," her father said, and left her to eat upstairs alone.

She hid the necklace from view, tiptoed upstairs, and kept the lights off to keep inconspicuous.

She bit her knuckle. A thousand questions and hypotheses ran through her head. Abandoning her food on her bedside table, she kicked off her clothes and jumped into the shower to rinse off.

How did showers work in Arkeh:na? The caves smelled a bit like smelly armpits, but all caves had their own special tang. Maybe they showered in that lake. Did they repurpose the water? Did they shower outside? Did they even shower at all?

Were there more communities like Arkeh:na in America?

Were they safe?

Were they okay?

With her hair still damp, she faceplanted into bed. The Grandmoeders had said that not many surface people stumbled across Arkeh:na. If that was true, how many other people knew about this Community?

She pulled out her laptop. Searching for 'CAVE PEOPLE' felt too wide of a net to cast, but typing in 'CAVE PEOPLE HISTORY IN UPSTATE NEW YORK' worried her. What if the government was tracking her now that she made contact?

Rolling her fingers over the trackpad, she typed in the question she wanted to know most: 'IS THE PRONOUN 'THEY' A VALID PRONOUN FOR A SINGULAR PERSON TO USE?'

It was.

Then she asked: 'HOW DO YOU COMMUNICATE WITH SOMEONE WHO SPEAKS A DIFFERENT LANGUAGE THAN YOU DO?'

A wealth of information popped up, and Avery took out her sketchbook and wrote down everything she saw. Within ten minutes, she'd written out complex notes that rivaled the ones in her English notebook. She found famous hermits living in caves, but they were nothing compared to Arkeh:na. She found Amish towns and African tribes that reminded her so much of the Community, but different. Little bits of cultures from all around the world had seemingly been mashed together to create what Arkeh:na had made for itself.

Just as she started her third page of notes, a screen popped up around her browser. Thinking it a virus, she went to close it. Then she saw the username.

xxCrossingRiverxx07.

That username, that profile picture of a wilted rose, Avery had nightmares about them. They'd once been a godsend to her. Late at night, fighting her feelings, she'd see her come online and get all giddy underneath the covers. As an oblivious eleven-year-old, she didn't realize why she made her heart flutter. Now she did, and it poisoned her veins whenever she thought about it.

But even so, she couldn't help but check up on Bridget. It was the reason her pictures by the fireplace had yet to be burned. They were all of her, posing with Avery like good friends did.

A conversation dinged underneath Avery's username, wondering_wanderlust101.

Hey.
Was what you said to me this summer true?

Avery made sure not to start typing so Bridget didn't know she'd seen her text. Because of Arkeh:na and Cameron, she'd mentally pushed aside the pain she hadn't yet confronted. She planned on never confronting it. What was Bridget doing, messaging her first? She never did that.

Avery typed:

> I'm sorry.
> You can forget about what I said.
> I was being stupid.
> We can be friends again if you want.

Bridget already started typing before Avery hit SEND.

> I can't forget.
> It's been messing me up.

She tried to type up a response to dissuade her, but Bridget typed faster.

> Are you really gay?

She stared at those four simple words, words she'd been too scared to think about since last summer. She'd tried to keep it a secret from everyone until her, her best friend, had asked if she liked anyone. Avery's answer was simple: her. Her laugh, her interests in writing for the school newspaper. She loved everything about her.

When she told her that, Bridget asked her father to come pick her up. That was the last time they ever spoke.

As Bridget began typing another question, Avery shut her laptop and buried herself in her blankets. To keep herself from crying, she prayed that when she awoke, she'd be back in Arkeh:na, deep underground where she could finally bury away these problems for good.

Chapter 7: Friends

Cameron crept to the *tunnle* wall and leaned their ear against the rock. As always, they heard a hum. A magical hum. An "I'm here, just find me" that all *gemmes* whispered when Cameron neared. Taking out their small pick axe, they chipped away at the softer dirt to gain access to the harder rock. They chipped away pebbles, spat out dirt that flew into their mouth. They dug a bit left towards the voice, then there: a twinkle of a *gemme*.

A blue twinkle. Yet another aqua. This marked the fourth one that day.

They held the *gemme* like a newborn baby. What did this color mean? Water, the ocean? Their eyes were blue, the left a little paler than the right. Avery had been wearing a blue shirt when they met. Maybe her favorite color?

They kissed it, waiting to hear what it wanted to say.

They felt a cough coming on, a typical occurrence in their body, but when clumps of dirt fell from the hole they'd just created, they held their breath. An earthquake? A collapse? Rare as they were, most of them resulted from Cameron's doing. Had they caused yet another?

They hadn't, and the world settled down with the *gemme* voices.

Securing the *gemme* in their pocket, Cameron ran out of the cave as quickly as their legs could carry them.

That night, they snuck back into the Main Exit *Tunnle* with an extra lantern. They wouldn't need it, but Avery would. Maybe, if she wanted to hang out in their den, they could light a candle for her, make her feel more at home. They heard Autreans still knew how to use candles.

Two days passed and the firebugs slowly flickered out.

After the second lonely night came and went, Cameron sulked back home. Why did they feel so disappointed? They'd never waited for somebody like this before, so anxious to meet someone new. They knew their Fader's absence and Moeder's distance left them a little awkward, not knowing the right words to say. Had Avery finally caught on? Had she realized that they were perhaps the least interesting Arkeh:nen down here? What if she started hanging out with other boys and girls their age and forgot about them entirely? She probably had loads of friends to pick from on the surface.

In the *ville*, yawning *shoppekeeps* were putting away their wares and kissing their neighbors goodnight. The *Centrum* was clearing out and the artisans had doused out their stoves. Claire was just boarding up her honey *shoppe* when Cameron passed by. They'd been keeping her honey jar on them in case Avery came back, but it'd been two days now. Others needed this delicacy more than they did.

Claire waved them over. "You're still up?"

"I've been restless." They handed her the bottle. "Here."

"You don't want it?"

Of course they did. How rare was it to indulge in honey purified by the psychics? Arkeh:nen food came in as either forest meat or berries. Sometimes scavengers borrowed Autrean food, but not many people ate it. The Grandmoeders didn't approve of tasting Autrean sweets.

Instead of being selfish, Cameron said, "Someone else can have it. Do you need help packing up?"

"Cameron, I'm fine, and take it. You *were* the one who introduced an Autrean to the Grandmoeders. I've heard they're quite interested in her. You're making them very happy."

Pride clouded their head. "I've heard."

"I've never seen your Grandmoeder so energized. You must be quite proud."

Cameron touched their face, hiding their bursting ego. Arkeh:nen dreamed of being minor influences to the matriarchy. To know the Grandmoeders were thinking of them in a positive light and not as a jinx made their heart beat faster than usual.

A clatter erupted near the *Centrum* pavilion, snatching Cameron out of thought. Someone yelled. Another shrieked. *Shoppekeeps* jumped with their wares in hand, wondering who'd just been attacked.

Cameron frowned. They recognized the yell, and they recognized the second voice just as sadly.

Basil had a boy named Patchway face down in a pile of pillows meant for lounging. Maywood was on her knees trying to pull her brother back, but Basil had a fight to win.

Storing the honey back in their pocket, Cameron ran down the *Centrum* steps and yelled, "Basil, knock it off."

At the sound of their voice, Basil yielded and let Patchway go. The little boy gasped for air and dashed down the steps to the underground layers.

"What's been the matter with you?" Maywood asked. "He didn't do anything to me."

"He pushed you!"

"I knocked into him. It was an accident."

Cameron helped Maywood back to her feet, then handed her her fallen cane.

"You can't let people walk all over you," Basil said. "You need to fight back."

"Fight back the Community? Are you mad? I don't like this side of you. You've been acting so off recently."

"What do you mean?"

"You snapped at Avery," Cameron said.

"And you've been unfixed. I feel like you're floating away from us."

"I'm right here," he said, opening up his arms. "You don't know what you're talking about."

"She's your sister, Cameron reminded him. "She knows you better than you know yourself."

Whatever they said struck a nerve, for Basil sputtered on a comeback and took off towards the silkworm huts. After fighting between what to say, he landed on what sounded like an Autrean swear and stuck his tongue at them.

Frustrated, Cameron copied the rude gesture and sat on the *Centrum* steps with Maywood.

"He won't do any better cleaning up," she said. "He's been so fired up lately. If he doesn't watch it, they'll fire him again."

"Did he get into another fight with your Moeder?"

"No. I think it's because of that Autrean girl."

"Avery."

"Yes. He was bad-mouthing her all day. I think it's because she's being seen as someone new and interesting even though she's Autrean. He...isn't thought of like that."

Basil's reputation in the *tunnles* stemmed all the way back to his Grandmoeder, Grandmoeder Nai. She'd persuaded their Moeder to live with a good, hard-working man, or someone she thought as good and hard-working. After their relationship stalled, bruises began appearing on their Moeder's face. She'd blamed it on her work in the *tunnles*, and no one argued against her. How could they? She'd been coupled by a Grandmoeder's wish. It couldn't be broken.

But then, one night, she ran away to the surface world. People didn't fault her for breaking such an important law. Knowing she'd never return, the Community silently wished her good luck.

But to everyone's surprise, the next afternoon, she was found sleeping in the *Centrum*. She said she couldn't leave her daughter, and that she wouldn't take her away from her homeland.

After a day-long discussion, the Grandmoeders overruled Grandmoeder Nai's wish, and Moeder Exia ended her relationship.

That next autumn, Basil had been born, a little brown boy with dark brown hair.

When Cameron had first met him, they didn't care that he looked different. He had a little tan, so what? Maybe he just played in the dirt too much. Up until his sixth birthday, they'd been the best of friends. Then he found out why people treated him differently than his sister. He followed the roots to people's whispers. He couldn't wash off the dirt. Then he iced over and cut up everyone who got close to him.

"I feel bad for him," Maywood said, "and our mother, but I'm sure you don't want to hear such stories."

"I do."

She smiled. It was forced. "I hardly see her anymore. She's been booking hour-long readings with your Moeder, and she's stopped sleeping in our den. I think she sleeps here most nights."

"Why?"

"I think she's planning on kicking Basil out."

Cameron's jaw dropped. "What?"

"She says his recent behavior reminds her of my Fader."

"But she wouldn't. She can't. *You* still live there, and you're sixteen. My own Moeder still lives in her birth den and, unless a cave-in forces me out, I'll be staying there forever, too."

Maywood smirked. "A cave-in that you'll create?"

"Hey."

She chuckled and stood up with her cane. "I should make sure he doesn't punch a hole in a wall and cause that cave-in."

"Do you need help? Do you want this?" They offered her the honey.

"I'm okay. Back when Basil was still a scavenger, he brought me bottles and bottles of honey. Now it tastes too sweet for me. Ask that Avery girl to bring us new food. The scavengers always tell us about how nice their food smells. I think it's time we try it."

Knowing she could get out of the *Centrum* by herself, Cameron went back to their den with their spirit a little heavier.

Technically, their Moeder still lived in their den, but Cameron's path hardly ever crossed hers. Catching her out of work was more of a miracle than having an Autrean land feet away from you.

Still, whenever they entered their *tunnle*, they slowed their steps, hoping to hear their Moeder cleaning their *gemme* cases or snoring in bed.

Aside from Nuvu, their den was empty.

She squeaked as they entered. She was hanging from her metal mesh, glaring at them upside down.

"It's alright," Cameron said. "She's not coming today."

She tried biting them, then stretched out her wings and turned around.

Cameron understood. They'd found her as a starving pup abandoned on a *tunnle* floor. Distrustful of humans, she slowly familiarized herself with just a handful of faces. To have someone new enter her home must've damaged whatever trust she had with them.

Before heading off to sleep, they paused to reconnect. They fed their firebugs honey and stripped to their skin-tight clothes. Then they knelt before their *gemme* collection.

Each *gemme* attracted different types of people. For instance, Cameron responded best to orange and yellow *gemmes*. They didn't discriminate and picked up any stone that called out to them, but these ones, they held a magic in their cut, a spark Cameron had been searching for for years.

They lay down in bed and positioned the *gemmes* on their chest.

The *gemmes'* energies slowly replenished them with positivity. Their coolness mixed with their warmth as they shared their stories through their skin. Their births, from specks in the rocks to their crystallization process, became years of magic destined to help Cameron right now in this moment.

They spoke, but gently, in a whisper. *"Don't worry so much about what's happening above or below the surface."*

"But I want to," Cameron whispered. "I want back control. It feels like the world's spinning."

"That's because it's becoming more difficult for you to breathe. You must tell your Moeder about your breathing problems."

Cameron coughed. "I can't. I don't want to worry her. I just want things to be calm again. Basil's upset, which's upsetting his family, but he's not opening up to us, and the Community's so high-strung—"

Energy pulsed into their arms, glueing them to their blankets.

The *gemmes* said, *"Earth was not made to be calm. It's why the wind dances and why waterfalls sing. It's why humans never stop growing, because they're restless. They want to live."*

"But Arkeh:nen don't grow. We stay small."

All the concentration Cameron was putting into their *gemmes'* conversation died when Basil walked in. He excused himself and knelt beside their bed, expecting them to drop everything and listen to him.

Doing just that, Cameron asked, "What's wrong?"

"Don't meet with the *Autrean* again."

"Why? They're not bad people."

"Yes, they are. You haven't met one before. You don't know how they act."

"You don't have to look out for me," they told him for the 1,001st time. "Did Avery seem dangerous to you?"

His fingernails dug into his rabbit-fur shoes. "Yes."

Cameron dropped their *gemmes*. They had to ask. Even if it came out awkward, they had to show him their support. "Basil, what's been going on?"

"Nothing."

"Come on. Maywood's worried. *I'm* worried. Maybe you should get your fortune read to clear your head."

"No psychic can understand what I'm going through. They all hate me, anyway."

Cameron took it like a slap to the face. "My Moeder doesn't hate you. She's only thought positive things about you."

"Then maybe *you* should get your fortune read. I never see *you* get one."

They tossed their head back with a groan, then threw it forwards just as quickly. "Hey, are you still wondering about your Fader?"

Basil's eyes widened. "How did you know about that?"

"Know about what? I'm talking about your birth Fader, the Autrean. If you're still curious, I was thinking Avery could help look for him. That's all. What did you think I was talking about?"

"Oh. Nothing." Fear clawed down Basil's neck. Realizing his mistake, he pinched off a piece of fur from his boot and twisted it until it disappeared in the air.

Cameron knew that look. They'd worn the same guilty expression the day they brought Avery down. "Basil?"

He turned away.

A guilty expression. The mention of his Fader. His lost job as a scavenger.

Cameron gasped. "Basil, have you been leaving Arkeh:na to find your Fader?"

Caught, he leaned out of the den to listen for anyone eavesdropping.

"*Basil*," they whispered. They still felt guilty *thinking* about going to the surface. The thought of breaking one of Arkeh:na's strictest laws had scared them into staying honorable.

"Don't tell anyone," he begged. "I'll stop. I won't do it anymore."

"But you're not a scavenger anymore. It's not allowed. How long have you been doing this?"

"A few weeks."

"*Weeks*? You got fired a month ago!"

"I know," he said, and rubbed his upper arms, no doubt feeling the Community's worriment creeping up on him. Whatever you did, be it something good or something bad, it always seeped back into the Community. It affected you, your Moeder, Grandmoeders both here and not. His Moeder had left, but for justifiable reasons. Could this be justified? If caught, would the Grandmoeders forgive him?

Cameron settled down the harshness in their heart. Of course speaking about Faders would get them like this. "What would you say if you found him?" they asked in a softer tone.

He shrugged. "What would you say to yours?"

58

"Mine's dead."

"Yours is *missing*."

What was the difference? Unlike Basil's Moeder, Cameron's Fader had announced his departure a day beforehand. He'd wanted to leave and was banished because of it. They should've felt grateful that they had no memories of such a man, only blurs of a face and the smell of river water. And his laugh. Soft and light, the exact opposite of their mother's.

"If I could," Cameron said, "I'd ask why he left, and why me and my Moeder weren't good enough for him to stay."

Despite not making a joke, Basil chuckled. "That's what I'd like to ask the Grandmoeders."

"What do you mean?"

"They *love* that Autrean girl. They want to know everything about her. Everyone is suddenly charmed by the idea of meeting an Autrean, yet here I am, and they hate me."

"They don't..." They corrected themselves. "Everyone's just confused right now."

"No, they aren't. She's a shiny new toy for them to play with, while I'm the second-rate *thing* they can't stand to look at."

Cameron gripped their heart. Is that how he truly felt? Second-rate? A *thing*? How could someone think so badly of themselves?

They collected their fallen *gemmes* and piled them around him. They even lined some on his leg, which he shockingly allowed. "I know they don't have much magic in them, but if they can help..."

Basil picked up an orange *gemme*. His energy remained stagnant.

They fought with themselves. What did he need to hear right now? What could help him out of this horrid state, if just for a moment? They said, "You're not second-rate. Not to me, and not to those who love you."

He lifted his head. A small ounce of color returned to his cheeks.

"Friends don't see friends like that."

A stab of pain, then a smile, a forced one like Maywood had taught herself to do. "Thanks."

"You're welcome. Do you feel any better? Please talk to someone about this, someone better than me. Talk to Maywood, okay?"

"I'll try," he said, then wiped a hand down his face. "I do love Arkeh:na. I love the people and their ways. I just keep thinking that, if I left, everyone would be happier."

"No, they wouldn't. You belong here. Just because a few older Arkeh:nen are prejudice doesn't mean you have to abandon the friends you have. When Avery comes back, I'll ask if she can track down your Fader for you, I promise."

"The Autre world isn't like Arkeh:na, Cameron. She won't know every single person up there. And don't bother. I don't like her. She's not good enough for you." He dusted off his knees and got up. "Don't tell your Moeder about what I've been doing."

"I have to tell her if she asks me, Basil. You know that."

A sickly look overcame him.

"I'm sorry. Maybe you can ask your Moeder for guidance, or mine. You can book a duel reading."

Basil scoffed at such a notion and waved them off. "See you."

They returned his wave until he left, then took out the aqua *gemmes* they'd excavated that week. If their Moeder asked, they wouldn't really tell her everything. Still, thinking that Basil was leaving his home to find another troubled them. If caught, he could be excommunicated from Arkeh:na, forced to live in the woods hunting for a nameless Fader.

They snuggled into their bear pelt. They didn't mind being the harbor for Basil's pain. They didn't mind acting as a counsellor for Maywood. If it kept everyone together, what harm did it cause? Best their energy be used on their friends rather than themselves.

The *gemme* in their hand twitched, causing them to lose it somewhere in their blanket.

"*Liar*," it whispered.

Hiding it away, Cameron instead took out their honey jar. They watched the gold drip down the glass. Right before it reached the end, they popped open the lid and took a sip.

Chapter 8: Lesson in Language

For a reason they couldn't quite work out, they awoke with Avery on their mind. She teased their dreams as a fairy, twirling through sky blue waterfalls and pansies, before taking their hand and bringing them into consciousness.

When Cameron awoke, they patted their blankets, first for her, then for their Moeder. They found neither woman, but did see Nuvu watching over them like an angel.

How strange. They never dreamed of people they knew, just faceless strangers in unknown *tunnles*. Avery must've been thinking about them somewhere on the surface.

They stretched out their sore joints and got dressed. As they went to their grub collection for breakfast, they stepped on something hard near their curtain. One of their aqua *gemmes* had rolled off its shelf. It rested against their excavating equipment, pointing out towards the *tunnle*.

"Alright." They picked it up and stuffed a grub in their mouth. "Show me where you want to go."

The artisans had just opened their huts for the morning. Pottery makers carried cups from the kilns as bat owners cooed for their bats. Cameron stood up tall to search for either Maywood or Basil and give them a good morning, but they stumbled across a strange scene: a completely deserted *ville*.

To make sure they weren't losing their sight, they checked inside one of the silkworm huts for answers. Two older Arkeh:nen named Berr and Hayes were threading silk into their ancient spinning wheels.

"Mornin', Cameron," Berr said. "I thought you'd be outside with everyone else."

"Outside where?"

Hayes smiled and pointed towards the Main Exit *Tunnle*. More than two-dozen Arkeh:nen were crammed into the *tunnle* opening like mice trying to squeeze into the same hole. They murmured as they stood on their tip-toes, trying to see something spectacular.

Cameron tripped out of the hut and ran towards the Exit.

Double the amount of Arkeh:nen were huddled inside. Some balanced their babies on their shoulders while others climbed onto higher rocks to see up ahead. No member of the Community acted this way unless one of two things happened: a person had died, or someone had brought down a treasure from the surface: a good roll of rope, glass.

A person.

Cameron darted through the crowd and made their way towards the center of it all.

Avery stood amongst the curious with her arms tight at her sides. She smiled weakly, a defense mechanism to disarm a threat. When she spotted Cameron, though, she relaxed and gave them a real smile.

Cameron smiled back. Not only was she wearing a new outfit today, she had their necklace still around her neck. She entangled her fingers through the twine as she waved.

They couldn't control themselves and ran into her for a hug. She smelled sweeter than last time, like she'd touched a spot of honey around her ears.

She didn't hug back. She stood there, speechless, and slowly, the awkwardness pushed Cameron away. They should've said something to her first. Of course she wouldn't have approved of something so abrupt and physical.

They rubbed the *gemme* in their pocket. Their hand came back sweaty. "I thought you'd never come back."

She said something in return.

"I still can't understand you."

She shifted her weight on her heels. "My...Moeder."

"Moeder? Your Moeder what?"

"Moeder..." She made a harsh X with her forearms, then pointed at herself, then to the top of the Exit hole. She pretended her fingers were walking down the decline.

"Your Moeder forbade you from coming here?" To say this, Cameron copied her hand gestures with a confused look, and she nodded.

Satisfied that she now had a trustworthy companion with her, the Community dispersed. Some eyes stayed on her, but the Grandmoeders had made up their minds. They wanted to see Avery more often, and if someone had a problem with it, they had to keep it to themselves. Or argue with their elders, like anybody would do that.

Like before, Avery marveled at the expanse of Arkeh:na. She turned in circles with a hand over her heart, her smile suppressed, too nervous to show off her true feelings.

Cameron picked the dirt out of their fingernails, then tapped her shoulder and pointed towards the *Centrum*.

They sat together on the best throw pillows filled with the fluffiest goose feathers. While she dug something out of her backpack, she looked up to the pillars and lanterns spiraling around them. The amount of awe in her profile left Cameron taking peeks at her behind her back. What was wrong with them? Was it because she'd dressed differently, that she smelled nice? Everyone in Arkeh:na dressed differently and smelled nice. Why had they noticed such details about her?

When she pulled out a book, they raised their brows. Not many Arkeh:nen could read, and Cameron didn't know how to draw. What good would paper do them?

Nevertheless, they swung around a *Centrum* lantern for her to see.

"Thank you," it sounded like she said, and opened to the first page.

Pictures of Autreans looked up at Cameron. They looked so lifelike that, for a naive moment, Cameron believed them to be miniature people and not just pictures captured in time, these "*fotos*."

Basil had explained this technology to them once before, about how Autreans could capture moments in time and paint them quickly with perfection. *Fones* could do it, as well as "*kamras*," but it looked like Avery had put these pictures here for safekeeping.

They felt around the *fotos*' corners. She had pictures of herself in broad daylight and of her sitting on an elevated, fancy-looking bed. In some, Past Avery stood next to two adults who must've been her parents. She looked to be six or seven in them, her hair curled just above her shoulders.

"Moeder," she said, pointing to the woman, "and…"

"Fader."

"Yeah. Moeder Juniper and Fader Ethan."

"And Avery," they said, touching her knee.

"And Cameron."

Their "ands" sounded so similar. Could they make more words like this? More questions? All Arkeh:nen had questions about Autrean life, and now Cameron had the perfect teacher to learn from.

"Fader?" Avery then asked. "Cameron's…" She raised her shoulders and hands, posing a question.

"My Fader?" Cameron asked.

She nodded.

"*He looked a lot like you*," was the most they'd ever gotten from their Moeder. Along with his name: Erik.

Without the Autrean words to tell her that, they copied what she'd done and made an X with their arms.

She frowned. "Sorry."

"It's okay."

She flipped to the next page and started sketching with her quill. She squinted as she drew, as if one lantern wasn't enough. They noticed that deep inside her shirt pocket hid her *fone*, now turned off to keep from blinding them.

She drew a few *gemmes*, then pointed to the real ones around Cameron's neck and made her questioning pose.

"*Gemmes*?" they asked. "Well, *gemmes* are…"

"Good?"

"'Good'? Did you say 'good'? Yes, *gemmes* are good. They heal us, protect us. They guide us when we're lost or scared."

"*Gemmes*...help...Cameron?"

Excited, Cameron took Avery's quill and drew a big smiley face next to her *gemme* drawing. They took turns scribbling more doodles around it, though theirs couldn't compete with Avery's. While shaky, her love of drawing shone through the page.

They spent nearly a half hour drawing together. Cameron drew rabbits and mice while Avery drew people and symbols. After they filled up two pages, Avery wrote out her alphabet in near perfect handwriting. Cameron had nothing to offer, so they tried teaching themselves her letters. They did their best, but things like "TVs," "cities," and "laptops" didn't and would never register with them.

"They're like—" She pretended to fiddle with something in her lap.

"Is it an object, or something like magic, like an idea you summon with your heart?"

She pressed her mouth in a line, thinking hard. While she thought, Cameron thumbed through her book.

"Wait—"

They saw something, though. Right before she pulled it away, they recognized a familiar face.

"Was that me?" they asked. "Did you draw me?"

Avery pressed the book against her chest. "Not good."

"Not good? What's not good?" Inching it out of her hands, they flipped back to the page and admired themselves in her style. Their eyes still looked too big and their hair had a lot of detail in it, but it was undoubtedly them.

"This's really good," they said. "Can you draw me again? *Draw me?*" they tried in English.

Avery laughed at nothing and yanked down her hat. "Eye," she then said, averting the question. "Why eye?"

Cameron searched for a nearby rock and readied their theatrical performance. They indicated that, in this story, they were smaller. They pretended to carve out some rocks on their hands and knees, improperly digging without the equipment they had now. They made a note to look up cautiously at the *Centrum* ceiling as if it'd collapse on them. Unable to change fate, they then let the rock fall gently against their forehead and eye socket. They faked a head pain and gave a few moans to end the retelling about their first cave-in.

Avery quietly clapped her hands.

Cameron played off of her energy with a hammy bow. "I got these from the collapse, too." They showed off their calf scar and the skin etched away by the Earth.

Avery pulled her legs to her chest, admiring Cameron's body. Before they got too flustered by that idea, she took off her boot and two layers of socks to reveal her naked foot. Pink scars cut up her shaven leg.

"How?" they asked, and made the questioning gesture they'd been using.

Avery folded her notebook into a V. She pretended her fingers were a person walking carelessly towards the edge. She made a quiet outcry as they tripped and fell into the V.

"You fell?"

She tightened her shoulders.

"You got stuck?"

"S...Stuck? Yeah, stuck. For—" And she said something that sounded like "thirty minutes."

Cameron understood. By how well she dressed and carried her pack, she looked able to walk the woods by herself, but only Arkeh:nen could safely maneuver in and out of caves, Earth's unforgivable zones.

After they drew and wrote to one another, Cameron took Avery on a proper tour of Arkeh:na. All the places they *could* visit—no unwarranted trips to the Grandmoeders' Den. First they showed her the silkworm huts and how they extracted silk to make shirts and shoes. They described the artistic process with their hands more than anything. As Avery picked up more and more words, they still had trouble with Autrean pronunciation. She had a talent for learning new languages. It didn't surprise them.

Next they walked her through the pottery huts, and then the bat and insect farms behind them. While she liked how each bat owned a little collar, she did not appreciate the process of boiling insects for food. She scrambled out of the hut when the worms began to squirm.

Knowing she didn't like crowds, Cameron skipped the *ville* and crossed the *Rivière*. Across it was the school they'd graduated from. It was one of the only buildings in Arkeh:na, two stories tall and built into the wall.

The halls felt so much smaller than they had a few years ago. Their old moccasin cubby would hardly fit their current pair. The smell remained, though, that fresh scent of mud and new clothes. They learned how to be an excavator here, and a good Arkeh:nen. They met Basil and Maywood here and learned about their new pronoun. While they explored, Avery peeked into a classroom where children were learning about proper cave safety. They ran when a teacher caught sight of them.

When they entered the *tunnles* where most people lived, Avery clapped her hands together. She asked the most questions here, particularly when it came to the den sizes and the drapery acting as doors. Every hole and ornament enchanted her, so Cameron proudly explained everything to her.

"We trust one another not to break in and steal our stuff," they said. "We're all a big family living in different rooms."

Avery smiled up at the multiple levels of Arkeh:na. Whenever they needed to cross a rickety bridge or scale up a ladder, her hands trembled and reached for Cameron. They didn't know why, but whenever she touched them on her own accord, they stiffened up, almost as if to impress her. They knew they slouched, so why didn't they want to act natural around her? They palmed the aqua *gemme* for answers.

As they crossed a bridge to the northern dens, two young children crept up around a pillar. They took cover like sneaky foxes. Cameron went to ask what they were doing when one of them yelped. Avery had noticed them as well. They stumbled over one another and wailed back to their dens.

As they waddled away, Avery heaved over and choked on her giggles.

Cameron laughed along with her. Ever since meeting her, they feared she didn't like showing too much happiness in front of others. Seeing her shiny teeth and the tears in her eyes made them want to keep laughing for her sake.

But then their body shut down. A burning charred up their lungs and scratched their throat. Their shoulders numbed. Their arms went cold. They held onto the bridge's rope as they coughed to get something out.

"Cameron?"

"I'm okay," they wheezed. "This's normal."

"No...Normal? No, no normal." She wrestled out a small, orange bottle with a white top from her backpack. She put it back, not what she was looking for, then pulled out another bottle. She shook out two blue rocks and pointed to her mouth, indicating that Cameron should eat them.

Cameron finished coughing into the crook of their arm. "You can't eat rocks."

She read the bottle's label, then offered it to them again.

Again, they pushed her away. "I'm fine."

A crackle rustled in Avery's bag. Still holding the bottle, she unzipped another zipper and took out the crackling box Cameron had seen in the Grandmoeders' Den. "Moeder."

"Your Moeder what?"

She pointed back the way they came, back to the surface.

"Are you leaving? Already? You just got here."

She tried a few words, none of which Cameron knew, then pretended to ring something in her hand. She mimicked the sound a bell made whenever a Grandmoeder wished to speak with you.

"A bell? Was your Moeder talking to you just now?"

"Moeder, bell, yes."

Sensing that she needed to leave right away, Cameron escorted her back through Arkeh:na to the Main Exit *Tunnle*. She walked more confidently than she had a few days ago. Cameron had only lit a few firebugs and, when they reached the end, she'd only hit her head once.

She stared up at the small crack of light at the end of the *tunnle*. Her toes scrunched up in her boots. In a defeated tone, she said something akin to "goodbye" or "farewell."

Cameron tried copying her accent, then said in Arkeh:nen, "I hope your Moeder lets you come down more often."

"Yeah," she said, but Cameron didn't know if she understood exactly what they were trying to say.

She took a step forwards, and they couldn't help but do the same. It felt odd, but they gave each other a quick hug before she ascended back up to the surface world.

As Cameron waved goodbye, something cool dripped down their chin. Careful so as not to stain their shirt, they wiped it with their finger.

Blood smeared against their dirty thumb.

They licked it back up, pretended it was honey, and returned to the comforts of Arkeh:na.

Chapter 9: A Wardrobe Change

The following week, Avery went to school like she hadn't a secret to keep. She paid attention in class and greeted teachers who greeted her first. She acted perfectly normal, the average eighth grader.

She wanted to cry the entire time.

To fight through it, she managed to skip her last period. She'd pleaded with her gym teacher to let her sit out in the gym hallway. She'd blamed it on period pains, and she told her mother that, because of school-related stress, she wanted to be picked up and forgo using the bus. She couldn't stand being in school and not Arkeh:na, she'd never last the thirty-minute bus ride home. Since her mother usually worked from home, she reluctantly agreed to be her ride.

Around her, students K–12 filled the halls with scuffling chatter. Sport teams and afterschool clubs divvied up into their cliques. Classmates she'd grown up with got close to her and gushed about their plans they had for the weekend. Scared of seeing Bridget, Avery kept her face glued to the hallway window. She'd yet to spot her mother's car between the yellow buses.

To calm down, she opened up her notebook. She'd printed out dozens of pictures to show Cameron, but she hadn't expected them to see her *drawings*. Drawings of *them*. She'd caught herself doodling them in class, but they were doodles, not finished illustrations. She had to do better next time. They must've thought her a terrible drawer.

Still, she smiled at Cameron's doodles. The shaky lines and messy handwriting told her that they didn't often hold a pencil. She even chipped off some dirt smudging the page. She'd secretly hoped they would've drawn her, but no. Just *gemmes* and smiling faces.

She'd never tell anyone about Arkeh:na. Who'd believe her, and who did she want to? Her parents didn't even know she caved as deeply as she did. If they found out and actually believed her, then what? She'd be whisked away onto television shows and interviewed for her school newspaper. While boasting did come to mind, she'd decided to keep this, like most parts of herself, a secret.

After all the buses left and the hall became less sporadic, Avery looked up to see her mother's car waiting impatiently near the curb. She had her phone to her ear, likely about to call Avery to tell her to turn around. As she guessed, her phone rang a second later.

"I'm coming out now," she said, and hung up.

Her mother's car interior contradicted her messy computer workspace. She vacuumed it every weekend, keeping the floor mats free of crumbs. Whenever Avery entered into the backseat, her mother would watch her to make sure she didn't track in any dirt.

"How was school?" she asked in an automatic manner. "Why do you keep asking me to pick you up?"

"I've just been overwhelmed."

"About?"

"Nothing much."

Knowing she wouldn't get much more from her daughter, she turned out of the parking lot into the town of Foxfield.

Foxfield's Main Street was comprised of two gas stations, a supermarket, a post office, Town Hall, and a church built in the 1780s. Town Hall reminded Avery of a place pilgrims would flock to to discuss the Constitution. The houses even more so, with their white pillars and brick fireplaces. Her family lived about thirty minutes away from it all, outcasts of their own volition.

"Right after you texted me, I got a call from your grandmother," her mother said. "Grandpa collapsed again while trying to clean the stairs. He's in bed now, resting, but your grandmother's trying to take care of the store by herself."

"Grandma usually *can* take care of the store by herself," Avery said, recalling every triumphant speech her grandmother had given her about running her own store.

"Not at her age, not anymore. I wanted your father to go check on them, but he's out working in the field, and then you called. I'm planning on staying there for a few hours. Do you have any homework to do?"

"Not a lot. Can you drop me off—?"

"No. No more hiking. You've never hiked this much before. Your grandmother needs us."

Thinking about how Cameron would've wanted to help *their* Grandmoeder, Avery conceded and planned on visiting Arkeh:na another day. Not that she didn't care about her grandfather. It was just that, whenever they came to help, they always told them to go back home. They sometimes got into fights about it. She didn't want to stress them out with unwanted worry.

Her mother drove through Foxfield's farmlands with lax movements. The forest towered above them on the left while cows and horses grazed on the right. Avery had always wanted to try their fresh produce, but her mother didn't trust the farm owners. Unless she went to her grandparents' store, she couldn't try what Foxfield had to offer.

Her mother slammed on the brakes so hard that Avery's head flung forwards, her back jumping off the seat. Someone had taken the turn quicker than she had and sped away just as fast. Panting, she cursed them out and went to grab her cane, which'd fallen to the floor.

"The light's green," Avery warned her.

"I know," she said, and made the turn.

Avery studied the tip of her mother's cane. Maywood needed one of these to walk around. Some Arkeh:nen had bandages over certain parts of their body that caused them to limp. Most of them looked her age.

"Hey, Mom? What's it like being hurt all the time?"

"Explain."

"I mean with your cane, and how you're not going to get better."

"You mean being disabled."

"I think."

She tightened her grip on the steering wheel. "Do you think your Lyme disease is getting worse?"

"No. I'm still taking my medicine every day with breakfast." She patted her bag, feeling for both her antibiotics and her regular headache medication. When Cameron had ruptured into that coughing fit, she'd almost given the former to them. She probably shouldn't have offered it to them, now that she thought about it. Who knew what

Autrean medicine would do to their body. "I'm just curious about how it feels. I've...been talking to someone at school who might've been born sick."

"So you're talking about a chronic illness. It's a sickness that lasts for months, like cancer or asthma. It can sometimes be cured or lessened with treatment and self-care, but it normally stays with you. A *terminal* illness typically results in death."

Avery slid into the backseat, intimidated by her mother's knowledge. "I think they have a chronic illness."

"Well, it's difficult, to say the least."

"Does it always hurt?"

"More or less. You just have to deal with it. Some people can't afford to. I was lucky. If I hadn't been wearing my seatbelt when I got into that car accident, I would've gone straight through the window and lost more than just my leg strength. That bear or deer—whatever I hit—sent me straight through the guardrail and down a ditch."

Avery watched the blur of green and brown fly by. "How should I go about talking about my friend's sickness?"

"Well, what sickness does she have?"

She. Even though she didn't understand it herself, Avery respected how Cameron chose to identify, but she didn't have the courage to correct her mother. Not wanting to upset her, she said, "I'm not sure yet. They...She coughs a lot, but she says it's normal. She's also really frail and pale, the same with the rest of her family."

"Does she take medication for anything?"

"I don't think so. They're really religious, I think. They're like a Wiccan."

"*Wiccan?* Like a witch? Avery, don't hang out with Wiccans, especially if they're sick. You know how easily you catch colds."

"But what if they're getting sick because of the environment they're living in, like their house is moldy or the air taste bad? How could I convince them to get help?"

"Avery, you can only do so much for this girl. Not everyone can pick up their house and move to someplace better."

"You and Dad did when Grandma and Grandpa opened up their shop."

Her mother caught her eye in the rearview mirror. "If you're so worried about her, convince her parents to do something about it. You can only do so much for someone who doesn't want to change."

Avery smiled bleakly at the thought of her trying to convince the matriarchy to move out of a place they'd been living in for more than 300 years. Hopefully Cameron would understand her before the worst happened. Spending so much time in those tunnels couldn't have been healthy.

"Here we are," her mother announced, pulling into the rocky parking lot.

Her grandmother's and grandfather's ma-and-pa shop was trapped in a snow globe of autumn decor from the 80s. Everything smelled so much of artificial cinnamon that she fully believed the floorboards were just flattened cinnamon sticks.

Cardboard cutouts of hand-drawn apples welcomed them at the front door. Real apples, pumpkins, and pears sat next to apple, pumpkin, and pear candles. Cartoon milk jugs chilled above the refrigerators, and cheesy knick-knacks of bears and bald eagles collected dust on the tables.

Her grandmother, Sun, swiveled on her stool behind the front counter. Her crochet needles poked out of whatever scarf or blanket she was currently knitting.

"Where's Ash?" her mother asked. "Is he in bed?"

"He's fine," her grandmother said, "though he called down saying he walked into our closet and didn't like what he saw. Said he was going to rearrange the summer and winter clothes before dinner."

"He should be resting. Didn't you say he fell?"

Ignoring her, her grandmother beckoned Avery over and kissed her cheek. "How're you doing, baby?"

"Grandpa's okay, right?"

"Of course he is, but since you're all here, let's go up and see him. I told you, Juniper, there's nothing to worry about. Old people fall all the time."

"You have to worry when old people fall. I'm telling you, I found this nice retirement home that's afford-able—"

"Marlows don't go into retirement. We work until we die, and then our granddaughters take up the family business."

"I'm not good at talking to people," Avery reminded her.

"You haven't learned anything from your mother. Juniper, baby, come up with us. I wanted to talk to you. Ash's worried about this mountain your husband's demolishing."

Avery scampered up the stairs before her mother and grandmother. She never minded waiting behind them, but her mother would yell at her to go up first, and her grandmother always shimmied a little quicker whenever she was making someone wait. That Marlow stubbornness had never reached Avery's branch of the family tree.

Her grandfather sat upright in bed so he could watch the TV better. They had a heating pad warming up whatever part of him ached the most. He had it on the lowest setting.

To combat the television's volume, he shouted, "Hey, Avery, girl. I didn't know you were coming down to say hello."

"Hi, Grandpa." She bent down and withstood one of his surprisingly strong hugs.

"How're you doing? How's that girlfriend of yours? Is she still giving you trouble?"

Avery blew out her cheeks. She'd told him several times not to call Bridget that. "She's doing fine. She became president of the newspaper club."

"That's great!"

"Ash, Sun said you fell," Avery's mother said, pulling up a chair. "You shouldn't be working when you're like this. You should be settling down."

Avery's grandmother handed her husband his medicine along with a glass of water. "He's fine."

"He's not fine. You need to relocate to a retirement home. You can't keep taking these stairs."

"I don't want to talk about this right now," her grandfather said in a harrumph. "Avery, tell me about school. You're almost a high schooler now. Do you like your classes?"

"I don't have a lot of classes with Bridget, so we've drifted apart," she half-truthed, "but I did meet someone new."

"You *met* someone?"

"They're just a friend," she corrected. "Their name's Cameron. They're, uh, a foreign exchange student from..." She couldn't think of a country off the top of her head, so she blurted out, "England."

"A Brit?" her grandmother asked. "I bet she has a cool accent."

Avery wanted so badly to correct them, but she held back. She hardly understood it herself; the older generations would just make fun of her. "They're into rocks and gemstones, stuff like that. We draw together."

"I heard she's Wiccan," her mother said. "Magic and witches and the like."

"Well, that just makes her more interesting, doesn't it?" her grandmother said. "Does she cast spells on you?"

Avery chuckled, then seriously considered Cameron owning a wand. They'd be into healing magic, for sure, magic that came from holding your hand or resting their forehead against yours.

"Oh, Avery, I found some more sweaters for you to try on," her grandfather said.

"No more sweaters, she already has too many," her mother said. "Half of her closet is sweaters, and most of them are from you."

"I don't mind," Avery said, and went to hunt them down. When her grandparents weren't busy running the shop, they somehow produced their own brands of clothes. New outfits and socks would suddenly appear in their closet, then magically find their way to Avery. The thick material kept ticks from eating her alive.

"They're on the stool," her grandfather shouted.

"I got them," she called back, and flipped through the designs. They felt as soft as the bear pelt in Cameron's den.

She paused. She hadn't seen any closets in the Arkeh:nen dens.

Coming out with a mountain of sweaters, Avery ran around the corner and said, "Do you have any more you don't want?"

"Why?"

"I want to donate them."

Escaping the house was easy with only one parent on watch. Sometimes she'd run into the forest, hang out in the trees for an hour, then come back without them even noticing. Sometimes she'd get a scolding, but it amazed her how invested her mother got with her work.

When they got home and her mother went to her working space, Avery took one of her boxes of clothes up to her room. When she came back down, she had her school backpack stuffed not with school supplies, but with as many sweaters as the zippers could handle. Adjusting the weight on her back, she casually climbed back down to the first floor and headed for the garage. "I'm gonna walk Oreo and Pumpkin for a bit. They looked antsy when we pulled up."

Her mother checked the time on her computer. "Be back in a half hour, okay? Your father's coming home late."

"Okay. See you."

"See you."

Even though she was in the clear, she shut the garage door quietly so it wouldn't creak and settled her dogs so they didn't bark.

After leashing them up, she opened her mother's trunk and heaved out the remaining box of clothes.

Getting to Arkeh:na with a full backpack, a heavy box, and Oreo and Pumpkin tested her coordination skills. Maybe next time she'd bring a wheelbarrow. They had so much junk in their attic, junk that could help a whole lot of people. Boxes, old mattresses—how would she smuggle a mattress up these hills? Maybe she could ask some of those "scavengers" for help, the hunters allowed to leave the caves. She felt so bad, just now thinking about being charitable. She'd make up for it now.

When she got to the Main Exit *Tunnle*, she tied Pumpkin and Oreo to a nearby tree. Neither of them trusted the cave anymore after they watched it swallow their owner whole. To them, the cave must've looked like the mouth of a giant beast.

"You'll trust it soon enough," she told them as she moved the boulder out of place. "Trust me, it's kind of fun down here."

Oreo whined and rested his head on Pumpkin.

Not many Arkeh:nen welcomed her as flamboyantly as they'd done a few days ago. Some turned their heads and hid behind their parents, but most of the Community had accepted her, or tolerated her.

Cameron hadn't come for her, though. She knew what their den looked like, but she'd forgotten which level they lived on.

Taking a chance, she walked down the crowded *ville* shacks and stuck her nose in one of the open *shoppes*. Beneath the hanging blankets were boxes of iron trinkets categorized by size. She spotted soda cans and pennies and even brass bullet casings someone must've scavenged near the hunting grounds. The *shoppe* next door sold purple gems, the other nothing but fox furs.

Behind the *shoppe* lay another row of shacks, and in that aisle, admiring some metal scraps, stood Basil and Maywood. They spoke in Arkeh:nen as they examined a piece of metal. Basil noted the quality—something about "forest," and "I" and "better"—and Maywood went to put it back when she saw Avery.

She beamed like the Sun bursting through storm clouds. "Avery!"

She gave the *shoppekeep* a piece of fur in exchange for the metal and came over. She spoke enthusiastically about something, then seemed to understand that none of it had reached Avery's ears. Cameron talked slowly and repeated themselves for her, but she still needed time to nail down casual Arkeh:nen.

Basil sized Avery up with his usual air of disapproval.

She didn't want to, but without the ability to speak their language fluently, she asked him, "Can you show me where Cameron's den is? I wanted to bring these to them."

"What for?"

"Well, my grandparents—my Grandmoeder and Grandfader—knitted these, but they don't need them anymore. I wanted to know if Cameron or any other Arkeh:nen needed them."

At the mention of her noble grandparents, Basil reexamined the contents of the box with a skeptical look, then translated for his sister.

"Oh, good," she heard her say. *"Come this way."*

As they walked, Avery mapped out the path in her head for future visits. Lavishly decorated dens became markers for when they needed to turn or cross a bridge. Some extravagant people became recognizable, like the man who wore nothing but a poncho and the woman with a monocle in her eye.

Some older teenagers mingled near the railings. When they passed a group of boys, Basil stuck out his tongue and greeted them with slaps to their behinds. One of them said something and pointed at Avery, making the rest of them, including Basil, laugh.

Avery lowered her head in unknowing shame.

Maywood said something motherly and rested her hand on Avery's back. *"Boys, boys, boys,"* she kept repeating.

They came to Cameron's *tunnle* in quiet footsteps. Cameron was still asleep, bundled up in their bear pelt, their *gemmes* emitting a soft orange hue around the room.

When Avery stepped inside, Cameron inhaled and smacked their head against the stone around them. They threw out a sleepy hand to retrieve a *gemme* on their shelf, a comfort gem.

"I'm sorry," Avery said. "I didn't mean to wake you."

At the sound of her voice, Cameron said something in alarm and crossed their bear pelt over themselves. Once they got their bearings, they addressed her box with a question.

"My Grandmoeder and Grandfader made these for me"—she pointed at herself—"but I don't need them, so I wanted to give them to you." And she pointed at them.

They coughed and crawled out of bed. "Me?" they asked, holding a sweater against their torso for size comparison.

"Yeah, for you. For Cameron. And everyone else," she added, feeling Basil's and Maywood's brown eyes on her. "You can share."

"Wow." They went to hug her, but stopped themselves short. "Thank you," it sounded like they said.

Avery didn't know what to say back. While she knew the Arkeh:nen words for "you're welcome," she felt a little spurned. Did they not like her enough to give her a hug anymore? Had she upset them by waking them up? Did they hate her?

She pushed those feelings away. She was back in Arkeh:na, with them, and that was all that mattered. "You're welcome. I was looking at some of these and thought this one would look nice on—"

Cameron struggled to lift the box by themselves. Both Avery and Basil dove in to help them, but they succeeded on their own and left their den with the box in hand.

"Cameron?"

They disappeared into someone's den, calling for them. Then the next den, then the next, until everyone in the *tunnle* had come out.

Cameron took to handing out every single scarf and sweater to one of their neighbors. Parents from across the walkway came over hesitantly and some of those older boys thought themselves too good to accept the offer, but

Cameron made sure everyone—everyone but them—received a gift, until the box was empty.

Chapter 10: Questions

Avery only visited Arkeh:na two times in the next two weeks. Something about being a "middle schooler" apparently made her life horrible. Traversing through "hallways" of judgmental "high-schoolers" who all "hated" her sounded awful. They couldn't imagine someone hating her, and knowing she had to "learn about subjects she'd never use in life" made even less sense.

Sometimes she had time to visit, she just didn't have the energy. Something called "Lime Disease" often made her tired and achy. Knowing those symptoms all too well, Cameron understood. They didn't complain that every time they woke up and didn't see her, their heart slipped into a dark hole. They bit their lip and stayed thankful for having her in their life.

But why? They could safely say she was their friend and they always liked spending time with friends. They ruled out her unique smell and hair, her outfits and personality. They liked all of those parts about her. Something more drew them towards her, something they'd never felt with another person before.

Maybe it was her hat. Not many Arkeh:nen wore hats.

On one of the rare days she'd come down, Cameron sat her down with her notebook spread between them. After a month or so of knowing her, they still couldn't fully *talk* to her. Her English matched about thirty percent of Arkeh:nen words. They understood the gist of it, but sometimes she nervous-talked, speeding through her thoughts until she started mumbling. They applauded her ability to understand them when all they did was mumble.

"*What...age...is Avery?*" Cameron asked. They shared a bowl of porridge that morning. Cinnamon sticks and dandelions bobbed in the warm goop. While Cameron couldn't scoff it down quick enough, Avery hesitated with every bite. After a back and forth in her notebook, Cameron found out that she didn't like eating dandelions.

Some aspects of Autrean life still baffled them.

After swallowing down a big bite, Avery held up her age with her fingers.

"I'm thirteen, too," Cameron said. "Me, same."

"Same? Really?"

"Really."

Avery cuddled deeper into Cameron's blankets. She said she'd never felt real fur before. When she discovered the pelt's empty eye sockets and snout, she screamed loud enough for Nuvu to fly out of the den.

"What...do you learn...in school?" she asked in Arkeh:nen, and tapped her brain.

"Life," they summarized. "How babies are made, how to care"—they cradled one of their pillows—"for them, how to scavenge, how to count, our history."

"No medicine?"

"Medicine? We learn about medicine, sure. Mushroom medicine, remember? And if you're a healer, you go to learn more about it under an apprenticeship. Why?"

"Your cough." She coughed a fake cough. "And Maywood's legs. I'm scared."

She mentioned this a few times, so Cameron explained yet again, "Cave sickness is normal to us. We have to withstand it in order to stay here."

She looked puzzled, and Cameron knew it wasn't from the language barrier. They didn't know how else to tell her this. They never met an Arkeh:nen who didn't have an injury or sickness attached to them. To stray away from such bizarre thinking, they asked, "What do you learn in school?"

She took to her notebook. The light from the firebugs shined on her black hair as she drew.

Between the lines, she drew open books, music notes, numbers with smiley faces around them, something that looked like her *fone* device, an apple, a cooking pan, and a paper with a pencil against it. It looked like a lot to remember, especially since she was planning on going to school for eight more years. Cameron couldn't imagine going for more than six in total. It made Avery's determination all the more admirable.

"Do you learn how to do readings?" Cameron asked. "Like future telling."

Avery cocked her head.

"Fortune telling?"

She shrugged.

"Psychic reading?"

"Oh, psychic?" she asked. "Psychic, right. No, we don't learn those things."

Cameron thought they heard her wrong. "You don't know anything about psychics apart from what you learned here?"

"No many psychic in my Autre world. No people believe it."

"What don't Autreans believe in?"

"Magic."

What did that even mean? Not believe in magic? Did they not believe in breathing, too?

Cameron gripped one of the *gemmes* on their necklace. A shivery feeling came over them. For once, they didn't want to hear what she had to say next. "Do you believe in magic? My *gemmes*, do you like them?"

She lifted out her necklace from underneath her sweater. She caught her reflection in the *gemme* facets.

Cameron's knee hopped. All this time they thought she'd believed in it, as if you couldn't believe in something so real. And personal. Not just to them, but to all of Arkeh:na. If she didn't believe in magic, if she thought they were just making it up...

She dropped the *gemme*. "Before I meet you, no. No believe in magic. No *gemme* magic."

"B-but what about now?" they stuttered.

She took in their room. "Arkeh:na is magic. All the *gemmes* and people are magic. I believe now. You make me believe."

Cameron sighed so aggressively that they needed to cough. Thank the Heavens. How could they have doubted her? Of course she liked magic. What person their age didn't?

They wiped their lips of spit. "So you've never gotten your fortune read before?"

"I don't think so."

"I have. You should get one done. When I was younger, all I wanted to be was a psychic."

"You, a psychic?"

"Right?" they said through a sigh. "My Moeder says psychics are born intuitive. She said I wasn't. I think I was, but I never argue." Oddly, the jump in their knee had yet to fade. Something about the conversation still needed to be said, something their *gemmes* wanted mentioned.

They stole another look from her. "Can I do one for you?"

"Do yes?"

"A psychic reading." Before they received her answer, they started prepping the area. They took out their strongest *gemmes* and laid them out on their lap. They found a piece of bark that'd act as their board. They didn't own tarot cards like their Moeder, but they did have sage they'd light during birthdays and special events. They lit two bundles and set them outside of their bed.

Avery pulled the pelt around her, giving them space. Her gaze nestled that familiar sense of stage fright in Cameron's head. They could talk to their *gemmes* just fine, but when faced with someone else's emotions, everything stalled. The magic dripped back into the Earth. Their Moeder could carve out someone's inner demons into something approachable. Cameron could barely figure out their own feelings.

They pushed their bangs out of their face. If they could channel any amount of magic from their *gemmes*, please let it be with Avery.

They closed their eyes and rolled the *gemmes* in their hands. They felt a little agitated. One dropped out and hid underneath the covers.

"It's okay," Cameron told them. "Don't be scared."

The edges cut into their palm. Confused, Cameron dropped them into Avery's hands. They tried remembering how their Moeder did this. "Feel the grooves on each side, roll them around, hear what they have to say."

Avery closed her eyes and did as told. Cameron watched for any eye flickers or jaw clenching. When the magic didn't come, she peeked an eye open and waited for further instruction.

Why did it never work for them? It came so easily to their Moeder. Even Basil had more spiritual power than they did.

Cameron took back the *gemmes*. She must've thought them a fool, trying to summon magic, something she'd only recently started believing in, and being unable to read a simple fortune. For a fraction of a second, they wondered if it even existed at all. If most Autreans could go about their day without confiding in a *gemme* or reading their fortune, did it exist outside of an Arkeh:nen mind? Should they give up and accept that magic simply didn't care for them as much as they cared for it?

They covered their mouth. What was wrong with them? How disrespectful, and in front of Avery, no less.

When they went to put away their *gemmes*, electricity snapped down their right side and shivered them with ice. It slapped them hard enough to make them gasp and search for what they'd done wrong.

They hadn't noticed it before, but Avery wasn't wearing her *beanie*. For the first time since they met, they saw her pure face unobstructed by fabric.

Lingering electricity stood Cameron's hair on end. "I don't think I did this right. Something went wrong."

She asked a question.

"I..." They tried to shake the dirt out of their head, but couldn't. There wasn't any. All that clouded their head sat in front of them.

Avery pushed herself into their bubble. "You okay?" she asked.

They pushed their sweaty back against their bed wall. "Where's your hat, on your head? I can see...more of your face."

They said it slowly so they didn't have to say it in English, and the gears turned in Avery's eyes. First through Arkeh:nen, then with the actual realization that she'd forgotten to wear the hat she loved so much. She patted for it and messed up her hair.

"It's okay," Cameron said. "You look just as nice without it."

She chuckled, a laugh that concealed rather than unveiled. It shattered whatever confidence Cameron had left.

Too lost to ask themselves, they asked their *gemme* a single question to help them better navigate these feelings.

"*Take her hand.*"

'*Why?*' they thought.

"*Take her hand and kiss her.*"

Their heart clenched. What? Why would they do that? Weren't they friends? Why mess everything up with their feelings?

"*You won't mess anything up.*"

They didn't want to.

"*Yes, you do.*"

They didn't deserve to kiss her.

"*Yes, you do.*"

They didn't. She didn't like hand-holding. She didn't like them like that.

"How can you be so sure if you don't ask?"

They balled up their *gemme* to quiet it. They adored these rocks. Why would they be sabotaging them like this?

"Something not okay?" Avery asked. "What do your *gemmes* say?"

They took a brief glance down at her hand. It was curled inside the blanket, the perfect place to be held.

If this didn't work, they'd be sure to gift these stupid *gemmes* to their neighbors.

Wiping their hand clean, they placed it over hers and waited for her to flinch.

She did, but not one of her normal flinches that sent her back. She inhaled slightly, stilled herself, then placed her other hand over theirs.

Their *gemmes* had been right. They'd known all along, this part of Cameron they'd been avoiding. They did want to hug her, and kiss her, and hold her hand. They wanted to be with her for however long they had left on the Earth. Too afraid of rejection, they'd wanted to live in total ignorance of her love rather than take her hand.

But that was all they could do, or allow themselves to do, right now.

They massaged the top of her hand. "Do you like this?"

She nodded.

"Really?"

Another nod.

They should've taken their hand away by now. Their sweat was sticking them to her. "Can I take you somewhere special?"

Her hand tightened over theirs, ready to follow them.

Not many Arkeh:nen used the gondolas for leisure anymore. Sometimes lovers did, but more often than not they just helped carry supplies across Arkeh:na. Their Fader had been a gondolier and therefore tarnished all the charm that they had, but maybe Cameron could revive this piece of Arkeh:nen culture with Avery. Young Arkeh:nen did try to make this trip once in their life with someone they liked.

They led Avery towards the Grandmoeders' Den and took a left instead of a right. They felt her tense up, but they ushered her away, their heart pounding just as fast.

They wondered if their Moeder ever took this trip with their Fader. They hated thinking about him now, but all they knew about love stuff came from them. Basil had never dated and Maywood said she wasn't interested in any of the girls she knew. They felt like, deep down, they had memories of their parents being close. Their Fader holding their Moeder in bed, them sitting next to one another and not saying a word. They couldn't imagine sitting with Avery and doing nothing. They had so much to learn from her.

A shout echoed off the wet rock. Cameron recognized the voice and, like always, they wished they hadn't.

Basil stood on a rickety gondola, holding a mooring pole as he shouted at Maywood. It looked like her legs had given out on her again. She sat on a low rock while trying to bring her brother back down.

"Why're you shouting?" Cameron asked.

Basil stepped off the gondola and rippled the water. "What're you doing here with her?"

They pushed his pointed finger out of their face. "What're *you* doing here?"

"He's trying out to be a gondolier," Maywood explained. "It's temporary, to try to find his place. I came down to see if he was hungry, and then he started yelling at me. It's getting worse."

"What's getting worse? I told you, everything's fine!"

"No, it's not."

"She's right," Cameron said. They didn't want to get involved, but they couldn't leave Maywood unsupported. They realized just then that they hadn't asked Avery to look for Basil's father. They deserved this argument for selfishly helping themselves instead of him.

"Why're you spending so much time with her?" he demanded. "I've seen the way she looks at you. She looks at you like a meal, and you've been acting different ever since you met her."

"Uh—" Avery started, but Cameron put their hand out. She didn't need her energy drained by this.

"Who cares how she looks at me? I...I look at her the same way."

It was like Cameron had hit him or something. He faltered backwards and rocked the boat. "Are you saying you like her?"

Their brain told them to say "no," but why? Was it so wrong of them to like her? They couldn't speak to her that well and had only known her for a few weeks, but they knew they liked holding her hand and feeling her fingers curl around theirs. "Yes."

"But she's an Autrean!" Basil reminded them.

"You are, too, Basil. It's not a bad thing to be."

"Yes, it is! You don't understand. Your Grandmoeder might like her and think she's interesting, but mine doesn't. Ours hates her. Arkeh:na has been unsettled

97

about this for weeks. You should bring her back home before something bad happens."

"Are you threatening her?"

"*Threatening* her? Are you serious? Why're you two suddenly so scared about what I'll do? I haven't done anything. I'm just trying to make sure this girl doesn't ruin what we have."

"She hasn't ruined anything."

"You're not a psychic—"

"Um—"

"Shut *up*!" he shouted, and kicked his gondola into the other docked boat.

Droplets of water splashed into the river. The boats rocked a ticking echo down the river. Once it faded out, Cameron, shaking with rage, went to chastise Basil for shouting at her. What gave him the right to talk to her like this? Why did he hate her so much? They could've talked out their differences, so why was he shouting?

But when they tried to speak, they couldn't. They couldn't defend her or shout for her. They stood there, stunned, emotions racking against their weak chest.

Without her hat, Avery used her turtleneck to hide her reddening face. She turned away to keep herself together, but she couldn't stop herself from breaking down and sobbing into her collar. "I'm sorry," she cried. "I didn't...I..."

Cameron's heart sped up in the opposite direction. They'd never seen her cry before. Why couldn't they move? As she gasped for breath, why did they feel just as breathless?

Maywood stood up quicker than Cameron had ever seen her move, put all of her weight onto her cane, and slapped Basil straight across the face. Then she took Avery's hand and stomped away.

Chapter 11: Answers

She couldn't stop. She thought her anxiety had gotten better, but after Cameron had held her hand in such a soft way, her nerves had been a wreck. They'd finally taken her hand in the way she wanted. Whatever their *gemmes* had told them finally pushed them her way. What more could she do than shake and pray they weren't playing a cruel joke on her?

Basil yelling at her for being with them finally tipped her over the edge and made her look like the biggest idiot crybaby in front of all of them. She didn't know what she'd done to make him so frustrated. Had she said something offensive, done something out of turn? Did she deserve to hold Cameron's hand as someone more than a friend? Did he just hate girls like her?

She didn't know Maywood that well, either, but that didn't stop the girl from defending her. Before Avery could ask where she was taking her, Maywood paused and yelled at Cameron and Basil to keep up. Cameron, sticking their nose up at Basil, followed them back into Arkeh:na. Basil followed with his shoulders hunched and head to the floor.

Maywood said sweet encouragements to Avery to keep her from sobbing. While not catching a lot, Avery heard, *"It's okay. I'll fix this. He's upset, but I know why. I'll help. It's okay.*" She reminded Avery of a mother, but she didn't know if it was because of her need to take charge or her cane.

She brought them back to Cameron's den. She offered Avery their bed, which she took to better hide her face. When Cameron and Basil finally arrived—they dawdled a few seconds behind—Maywood sat Basil in the hole next to Avery.

Avery squirmed into the corner of the bed. Why next to her, his number one most hated person above and below the surface? She hadn't heard a lot of what he'd spat out at her near the gondolas, but she'd heard enough. The spit that hit her face made his opinion of her clear.

Maywood squeezed in beside Avery. "*Apologize.*"

Avery went to open her mouth, but Maywood silenced her and waited for someone else to speak.

Basil scrunched up his nose in defiance. When Maywood reached for her cane, he said something in Arkeh:nen, then said in English, "I'm sorry for yelling, but not for what I said."

"*What was that last part?*" Maywood asked. "*Be sincere.*"

"*I was. I said I'm not sorry for what I said.*"

"*Why're you so mean to her?*" Cameron asked. "*What did she do to you?*"

"*I think I know,*" Maywood said.

"*What do you know?*" Basil asked. "*You don't understand.*"

"*She's a sister,*" Cameron pressed. "*She knows things. Feels things.*"

Basil slouched against the wall. He stared into the blankets and pillows, unblinking and stern.

Breaking their tension, Maywood said something without hesitation and without malice.

Whatever she said stabbed him in the heart. He accidentally kicked a piece of rock out of the wall and sputtered out ridiculous questions.

"What did she say?" Avery dared to ask.

Cameron picked at their head scar. Discomfort reddened their face like a rash.

"Don't," Basil warned. "Wait—"

"He likes me."

"*Liked*!" he corrected in English. "Past tense! You're a friend now. Just a friend."

Avery's stomach turned. "You like them, too?"

When "too" left her mouth, Cameron lifted up their head. Sweat started forming around their hairline. Now they just looked ill.

"No!" Basil said, raising his voice. "As kids. School kids. They...We're friends now, right? Only friends."

"I don't think so," Maywood said.

Basil looked between all of them, desperate to stay above water. *"Why're you doing this to me? I just hate Autreans. I want to protect Cameron from them."*

"You don't have to," Cameron said. *"What she and I have—"*

"Is what?"

"Not yours."

They argued back and forth, breaking between the two languages. Basil raised his voice. Cameron's face reddened. Maywood played peacekeeper.

Avery had pegged down Basil's frustrations on things she didn't understand, but the holdback in his tone to be both accepted and ignored, she understood that perfectly.

It didn't excuse the way he treated her, but she knew how different she acted when this'd happened to her.

When the conversation broke into silence, Avery mustered up the courage to say out loud, "I'm the same way."

The den quieted. Maywood rested her hand over Avery's back.

"I don't have friends," she continued. "I only keep my phone on me to talk to my parents when they're not busy. It's been hard to make friends."

"Me," Cameron said. "Me, too."

Even though she wanted to, she kept her eyes on anything but Cameron. "I had one friend back in middle school—from the past, when I was younger—who I liked." She pulled up a picture of Bridget on her phone. "I liked her so much that it hurt to keep those feelings from her. One day, I told her how I felt, and she..."

She stifled back a few tears before they fell. She looked so happy in those pictures. "She didn't like me back. She said it was wrong to feel that way and to never talk to her again. She was my best friend. Now I have no one. I have no friends, my parents are always working. I have nobody I can go to for help. But then I found Cameron."

The tears sunk her head into her knees. "I've never felt so happy to be myself around someone before. I feel safe. I feel *happy*. They like my art and don't make fun of me for what I do. Basil, you remind me so much of myself back then, so scared and alone, unable to figure out what was wrong with me. I'm sorry I was the one to put you through that kind of pain. I didn't know."

Maywood fully embraced her, allowing her to cry into her shoulder. Basil kept staring into the same direction.

Avery didn't know what Cameron looked like or was feeling or if they'd understood half of what she'd gushed out, but she had to say it.

Basil leaned over and took the phone out of her hands. He stared at Bridget's picture with a solemn expression, then clicked through more photos, likely finding more of her. "It hurt."

She nodded into Maywood's shoulder.

"It was...empty?"

With Bridget's rejection still rotting inside of her, she kept nodding. "I'm sorry. If I'd known you and Cameron used to have something..."

"Don't," he said, interrupting her. "I never had it in the first place." He handed her back her phone. He'd turned it off for her. "I'm sorry."

"Thank you."

He picked a scab off of his cheek. "Honestly, I don't know many Autreans. I think they're bad because of my Moeder. I think they take away Arkeh:nen and break families apart. From what they do in the mountains, they cut trees and cut animals. I don't like that. I didn't want that for Cameron, but now..." The scratching deepened. "I get it. I understand. I was...too mean, to you. I shouldn't be. You are good for them. Too good."

He spoke to Cameron in their language, then crawled out of bed. "I'm sorry I say you don't belong," he added to Avery. "I think you do, with Cameron, with us. You belong."

She didn't know why, but that made her ugly-cry into Maywood's shoulder for almost a minute. Out of all people, it was Basil who finally made her feel accepted by this group of people, her friends.

When she finished, Maywood said, "*Sorry about this. I hope you can forgive him.*"

Avery sniffed. "*I already have.*"

With a nervous bow, Basil left with his sister. Avery had just enough time to return his wave before Cameron collided into her and hugged her.

"Sorry, sorry, I'm sorry. No sad, no do that more."

"I'm okay."

"Sorry, sorry, don't cry."

Avery patted their back like a baby. Their eyes looked glossier than before.

"Hey." She wiped their eyes with her thumb. "You're not supposed to cry, too."

"You...sad. You are sad." They switched to Arkeh:nen. "*I'm sorry about Basil. I never knew. If I had, I would've said something to him.* He *should've said something to* me. *My Moeder was right. I'm not very intuitive.*"

"I had a feeling he liked you, just not so much."

Shaking that off, they hugged her again. Even though they stood under five feet tall, in this moment they felt taller.

They held each other that way for minutes acting as hours. It could've been more; she didn't keep count. She longed for a moment like this with someone like them. She didn't expect to cut through so many brambles to reach it, but she wondered if everyone needed to when they opened their heart up to someone they trusted.

"*Is this okay?*"

"*More than okay.*"

They lifted their head and gave her that look again. Eyes half-closed, their injured one closed entirely. When they moved forwards, one hand on her leg, the other on her hip, Avery moved back to give herself more time—Was she doing everything right, did she smell, was she misinterpreting this as something more or less than what it actually meant? But when their breath kissed her parted lips, her brain fogged over.

The kiss came slow. Neither of them seemed to know how to kiss. Avery had only practiced so much with her pillow before she embarrassed herself, and Cameron had this need to push out their teeth and dance their hands over her arms like clumsy spiders.

It was more than she ever imagined. She didn't want it to stop. She thought she was weird because she never crushed on celebrities or singers, but this was the reason why. None of them fit her standards. None of them loved her like this.

When she pulled back, she allowed herself to fully indulge in her feelings. She didn't feel guilty about it. For once in her life, she let the butterflies in her stomach flutter eternally, hoping that they'd never land on the branches encasing her heart.

Cameron led her back to the corridor where the *Rivière* narrowed into a smaller river. The long boats bounced between one another, absent of a steerer, leaving them alone with the sound of calm waves.

"What's this for?" she asked in Arkeh:nen.

"Nothing but a ride," they said, and unhooked a firebug lantern from the wall.

Avery steadied herself as she stepped into one of the wet gondolas. Cameron stood in the middle. Her and their combined weight did sink it down a bit, but it managed to bob in the water without capsizing.

Cameron kicked off the rocks. They didn't have an oar with them, but as soon as they were about to hit the wall, they grabbed hold of a wooden peg near their head and steered them away. A few feet ahead and another stuck out, illuminated by blue and purple rocks. Cameron caressed them before steering the boat back into the middle of the river.

Avery watched them without fear. She didn't care where the river led her or what she and Cameron had just become. With a newfound smile, she let the river guide her down an unexplored path.

Chapter 12: The Oak Tree

"You say it like this," Avery said to Basil, then added a whole bunch of complex English words that Cameron didn't understand. They all sat together in the *Centrum* that day, they, Avery, Basil, and Maywood. Maywood had gotten out of work early with Basil, and Cameron had just finished up scouring through the *tunnles* before Avery came down to visit.

They didn't mind her getting to know their friends. After crying over her shoulder, she'd become closer to Maywood and joked with her in Arkeh:nen. She and Basil had finally come to terms with how they felt about each other and had formed a brother-sister relationship more topsy-turvy than the one Basil shared with his own sister. When Avery said a perfectly fluent sentence in Arkeh:nen, Basil came at her with a flawless phrase of English. Or what had to be flawless. Cameron had yet to get a handle on the adverbs.

They tore off their morning beetle's head, chewing their contempt into their cheek. It bugged them in the most childish of ways. It was the main reason why they didn't want to plunge into this type of love. They hated how they got with people they liked, be them friends or acquaintances or friends of acquaintances.

They wanted to be there for them for everything they needed. They wanted to solve their problems and help them through terrible times.

They wanted to be the only person to do that.

And if they had a girlfriend, they wanted her all to themselves, and they hated that they had to face this selfish, childish mindset of theirs.

Maywood bided her time knitting a pair of slippers for an upcoming baby. Whenever Cameron tore into another beetle, she giggled to herself.

"If it makes you feel better, I don't understand half of what they're saying," she said. "I'm not very equipped at learning new languages like Basil is. He only learned it to one day speak with his Fader. He listened to hikers and men who drill into the mountains."

"We should be practicing it *together*. I want to learn it, too. Basil already knows it."

"Then ask her."

Something Basil must've said prompted Avery to laugh out loud. When he saw her reaction, he chuckled back and playfully hit her knee.

Stuffing three whole beetles in their mouth, Cameron crawled over to them and shook Avery. "What did he say?"

"Something about a cave-in. You made it?"

"It was an accident! Basil, don't tell her this."

"They were upside down in the cave for hours," Basil explained. "It was pretty funny."

"Yeah, but not when it was happening."

Still, Avery kept snorting until she pulled something out of her pocket. It was one of their orange *gemmes*. "Basil tells me its name is a color. You call them orange *gemmes*, right?"

"Yeah," they said simply. What else would they've called it?

"I think it's called citrine. It's what Autreans call it. A lot of your *gemmes* are different cuts of citrine."

"Yeah," Basil said. "I once snuck into an Autrean store and read a book about *gemmes*. I saw this *gemme* in it, I just didn't know how to pronounce its name. English words are difficult to read."

"No wonder you got transferred," Maywood said. "First talking with Autreans, then going into their stores."

"But no wonder he knows so much," Avery said.

Cameron reevaluated their most prized *gemme*. All this time they'd been calling them by their colors. How many citrines had they collected over the years without ever knowing it? What about the red *gemmes* and brown *gemmes*, the green and blue ones? Did they have names, too?

Avery probably had the names for them.

"Avery," they said, "do you want to come collect *gemmes* with me?"

They didn't have to translate it into English for her to understand. Basil and Maywood got it just as clearly, because they became rigid at the invitation.

"What?" Maywood asked. "Did you say *gemme* collecting?"

"You can't do that," Basil said. "Even when I go into the caves, I get bad looks from the Community. To bring a fully Autrean girl there would make them mad."

The caves, the uninhabited parts of Arkeh:na, held a sensitive place in the Community's hearts. It was where they excavated *gemmes* and where the *Rivière* flowed in from the mountainside. They were considered the most magical depths of Arkeh:na. Children under thirteen weren't allowed in, and only trained excavators like Cameron could properly explore their niches without tracing their *kaart* scars for guidance.

"I think she can see them now," Cameron said. "She's been in my bed, ridden on the gondolas, *and* visited the Grandmoeders' Den. Seeing the uninhabited caves might finally seal her in as an Arkeh:nen."

"I'd like that," Avery said.

"You should ask around, just to be sure," Basil said.

Cameron cast aside his concern. Jealous as he might've been, they wanted to spend alone time with Avery. Just once, they wanted to think for themselves and be with her, their new girlfriend.

They sat up on their bad knees and took her hand. "Come with me."

"Which *tunnles* are we going to?"

"None. First, we have to stop by my den."

"Cameron," Maywood warned.

"It'll be okay. I'll be with her the entire time."

"Stay close to her," Basil said. "She doesn't know the caves like you do. Be safe."

They would be. They worked in the caves multiple times a week. It wouldn't make sense for the caves to accept them and not Avery, someone who respected the Earth likely as much as they did.

After reaching their den, Cameron strapped on their backpack and tied a lantern around a sturdy walking stick. Sometimes they needed one if they were planning long excursions into the caves, and Avery might've needed one if she got too tired.

"What is it?" Avery asked, hovering at their den's entrance. "Caving?"

"Caving is like getting lost on purpose and not being afraid of what you'll find."

"I'm a bit scared."

"Of what?"

"Being trapped."

"You won't get trapped. I'll protect you." They smiled. "If you get scared, you can hold onto me."

"That's a lot."

"A lot of what?" They tickled her sides until she squeaked out her fear. Then they caught Nuvu hanging on their metal mesh. "You wanna come?" they asked her. "Caves, Nuvu. Wanna come?"

She nibbled on her hooked thumb, thinking it over.

"You're gonna be awful lonely here by yourself. I'm planning on spending a *long* time in there with Avery."

Sensing their playful tone, Avery made a cooing noise and reached out to her.

She chirped, but made a move to come closer, interested to see if she had any grubs.

Cameron took out a fried beetle and placed it in Avery's hand.

Nuvu clicked, cocked her head from side to side, then swooped down and ate cautiously from Avery's hand.

Avery held back her smile at Nuvu's acceptance.

"She likes you!" Cameron said. "She accepted you. She never does that for people."

"She likes me," Avery said, relieved.

Cameron side-eyed her. *"Maybe...maybe she'll let you sleep here, too."* They dropped it semi-casually, pretending they hadn't been hoping for it for the past week.

Avery just smiled and made her way out of the den.

Cameron was sure they'd said that right in English. Whenever they spoke it, they worried about saying something wrong or hurtful, but it didn't seem like they could do anything to hurt her.

They took their favorite route to the main caves, but it also meant taking her through the more deserted parts of Arkeh:na. They hadn't meant it in a bad way; they didn't mind who saw them taking her down here. It just made sense, and they didn't want anyone to question them and make Avery feel bad about something she shouldn't have to feel bad about.

Keeping their steps light, Cameron quietly led her through the dark entrance of the caves.

Her grip tightened around their hand. Without the Sun, the *tunnles* must've been an experience for her. To help her, they kicked rocks from their path and kept her close until the first cave opened up to them.

They wondered if she felt more at peace in these caves than in Arkeh:na. As soon as the air cooled and the Arkeh:nen noise trickled away, her grip loosened. She looked less and less at her feet and craned her neck up to the steep, cramped walls slick with water.

They led her north to the more scenic caves. Here, the walls expanded for more air. Pools of water flowed around stalagmites and other rock formations. Ancient logs held up parts of the walls, but most of the rocks held themselves up with aged pride.

Wobbly bridges helped them cross the wider abysses, yet Avery still held onto them as if she didn't believe the caves would like her.

"It's okay," they said as they crossed a small bridge. "Something would've happened to us already if the caves didn't like you."

Her eyes traveled back down to the foot-sized holes in the bridge. "This's your job? You do this every day?"

"Yeah, it's fun."

"It's dangerous."

"I should excavate some *gemmes* for you. If you hit the walls right, they shake."

She ducked down as if Cameron could predict the future.

When they touched back down to solid ground, Cameron followed a trail of water that would've led them to the gondolas. Their steps echoed off one another's. "It's not that bad so long as you know where you're going. See these?" They showed her their newer *kaart* scars. "I helped make these *tunnles*. They're still tight, so we won't go down them."

"It reminds me of when I get stuck in the rocks."

Cameron slowed down. "Do you want to head back?"

She shook her head. "I want to see more."

The northern caves winded into illuminated paths, bright *gemmes* shining with joy as they lit their way. Nuvu, who flew back and forth through the caves, landed on the brighter *gemmes* to hunt spiders and cave flies.

"Oh!" Avery pointed up ahead to a pool of water cut into the wall. The miniature stalactites and *gemmes* on the ceiling perfectly mirrored themselves in the water, creating the illusion that there was no water at all.

Cameron nudged up against her.

"Cool," she said. "How do they shine?"

"From magic."

"They're pretty."

"They are." They ran a finger through the still waters. "Can I show you something prettier?"

Trusting them, Avery followed their way.

After taking the prettier routes and watching her eyes sparkle in the ponds, they came up to the site. No Arkeh:nen considered it sacred or magical, but knowing Avery, they knew she'd find it breathtaking.

Her shoulders drooped like the tree's mighty branches. Before them stood a large oak tree. It somehow found peace growing within these caves. Its branches stretched towards the tiniest opening in the ceiling, which let go a single stream of sunlight. Flecks of snow glittered across the leaves struggling to keep on the branches.

Avery touched the tree's bark. "This is amazing. *Cameron, this's so pretty!*"

She said the last part in English, but Cameron had memorized the phrase. "*I know*," they said. "*It's pretty, like you.*"

Again, she didn't respond. Their forcefulness to compliment her didn't sound right in their ears, but they wanted her to know that saying such things was alright when they were alone. Maybe they were trying to convince themselves of that.

They looked up at her, remembering how tall she looked when they'd first met. It took a few moments, but she finally looked back, snagged.

They took her hand. They tried to think of how to explain their feelings to her in both Arkeh:nen and English. They wanted to sound poetic and lovely. They wanted her to *get* everything that was stored in their brain, but they didn't have the words.

Standing up on their tiptoes, they leaned forwards and kissed her.

Unlike last time, instead of panicked admiration, Cameron felt wrong. Was this right? Should they have pulled away by now? They'd never had a girlfriend or boyfriend before. Did people kiss this often, or were they making her uncomfortable again?

They pulled back. "Sorry."

"Why?"

"You don't like it."

Without explaining herself, Avery leaned down and embraced them. Her arms wrapped around their waist and hoisted them up. It forced them back on their tiptoes to meet her height.

"I do like it," she confessed. "I like it, a lot. I feel better when I'm with you. I like hanging around you."

Their heart pounded against hers. This sounded like a break up.

"I'm getting more confident around you," she continued, "but I have trouble with things. Personal things. Kissing is scary for me."

"Should I stop?"

"No. You're helping me through it. I don't want to be afraid anymore."

Knowing she wasn't breaking up with them, Cameron wrapped their arms tightly around her. They never thought they'd be scared of love. What were they so afraid of? Being close to her? Getting caught with her in their arms? Why?

"I want you to stay here," they whispered. "I want to see you when I fall asleep and find you by my side when I wake up. I want you to become an Arkeh:nen."

She was already shaking her head before they finished. "I can't. My parents would...I have school. I have my family."

They knew that. They knew it was impossible. It was like asking them to abandon Arkeh:na in exchange for the surface world.

That way, though, they'd get their wish and spend more time with her.

It wouldn't have been so wrong, right, to spend one day outside Arkeh:na? If it meant being with her...

Avery pulled back.

"What's wrong?" they asked, but when they asked, they looked up at her, and when they did, they saw what she'd seen.

A pebble fell between them. Then another. Then three more.

Cameron had only lived through one of these twice. They'd been taught what to do as a child, but no one truly knew how to act during the first moments of a cave-in.

An avalanche of rocks caved in around them. The world crumbled. The walking stick cracked. Their hands moved before their brain did and shoved Avery away just as a tower of rocks cascaded between them.

The cave reformed itself in a turbulent storm. Dust and dirt choked the air. Cameron was pushed against the rock with the strength of a bully, and all they had was their backpack to protect them. They knew it wouldn't save them, but they taught you this as a child for a reason. It made you feel safe in a world you couldn't control.

It always scared them how calmly a cave-in ended its rage. It took out so much, killed so many, then disappeared into the cloudy air as if it never happened. When its energy fizzled away, Cameron couldn't breathe. Rocks clogged their throat and lungs. Their lantern was gone. Their chest had a heartbeat. It took Avery screaming their name for a fourth time before they moved.

A new wall sectioned them off from one another. Cameron leaned their ear against the wet dirt and listened. "Avery?"

"*Cameron!*"

Their heart skipped. She was alive. Whatever had befallen her, whatever they'd done to make this happen, she'd survived. The caves had spared her.

"Cameron, help! Help me! Trapped!"

They felt up the wall. It'd take hours for them to dig her out by themselves. But if they called for help...

"I-I'll get you out," they promised. "Wait here."

"No, don't leave me alone. Please!"

They stumbled back home. The realization that they'd caused another collapse didn't hit them as harshly as Avery's safety did. They needed to get her out. They needed to right this wrong.

"*Cameron!*"

They needed the Community to forgive them.

Chapter 13: Cameron's Choice

What should've been a fifteen-minute sprint back into Arkeh:na stretched out into a half-hour slog. The cave-in had destroyed the quickest route back into Arkeh:na's main levels. The main *tunnles*, buried. The shortcuts, destroyed. It kept Cameron in the dark about the Community's safety and lessened Avery's chance of being saved.

They felt more broken than the caves they'd just destroyed. What were they thinking? *"Spend one day outside Arkeh:na?"* Had they become a heretic like their Fader? No wonder the caves had tried to kill them. They deserved it for thinking such thoughts.

But Avery didn't. She didn't deserve any of this.

When they finally reached the main layer, coughing and wheezing on the poisoned air, they entered into a world of disorder. The *ville* was abandoned. Arkeh:nen ran about with no direction. Pieces of the wall and ceiling were crumbling and the *Centrum* had lost one of its pillars, leaving their Community tilted.

The wall sharing the silkworm huts and Grandmoeders' Den had collapsed. No light from the outside came through, but a steady slope had slipped into the Community. The school beside it had barely been saved. Moeders and Faders gathered as many children as they could away from the debris. Excavators helped dig out the affected huts. The rest watched on, helpless.

Two workers pulled out a struggling Maywood. She'd lost her cane and was trying frantically to get back to the silkworms.

"Get him! Get—*Basil*!"

Cameron stopped running. They'd tried so hard to be the perfect Arkeh:nen. They loved their people. They respected the Earth. Why was fate punishing them so harshly? Did they truly deserve this much pain?

A woman came out of the ruined hut coughing. She was bleeding from her head and had Basil draped over her shoulders.

"Moeder," Cameron breathed out.

Their Moeder laid Basil on his back, careful about his right leg. It didn't look broken, but it was bruised and puffy from an injury.

Basil moaned and covered his face in shame. "I'm sorry. I went back for Maywood, but I couldn't find her."

"It's okay," Cameron's Moeder said. "Just stay calm."

Around Cameron, whispers spread.

"How did this happen?"

"Is anyone else hurt?"

"How're the Grandmoeders?"

Cameron's knees buckled. They had no proof that they were the one responsible for the cave-in, but the last two collapses had been because of them. Once because they'd excavated a *tunnle* wrong, the next, absolutely random, just outside of their own den.

They covered their mouth with both hands. Just when they thought they'd pass out, Avery's screams rang through their head, reminding them of why they were here.

"M-Moeder!" They ran up to her. "Moeder, Avery's in the *tunnles*. She's buried. I knew I wasn't strong enough to dig her out, but if we don't get her out soon—" They doubled over in pain. They coughed out something dark, maybe blood, maybe dirt, before their Moeder touched their shoulder.

They tried controlling themselves before acknowledging her kindness. She didn't touch them often.

"Where is she?" she asked.

"In the caves."

"*Where*?"

They swallowed back hard. Their Moeder hadn't taken their hand off of them. "Near the oak tree in the northeast corner. I just wanted to show it to her."

"You brought her into the caves?" one person asked.

"She's Autrean," another said.

"Not everyone can be accepted by the caves."

"Do you realize what you've done?"

Cameron could no longer bear it and slipped to their knees in humiliation. Boulders larger than all of Arkeh:na compacted them into the worthless, magic-less *gemme* they were. Born to a Moeder psychic, deserted by a heretic Fader, and disowned by the very *gemmes* they loved, they belonged nowhere near the home they destroyed.

A hush fell upon the crowds. Cameron's Moeder finally took her hand off of them as she rose to see something above the crowd. Cameron stayed on their knees where they belonged until their undeserved curiosity overpowered them.

All five Grandmoeders stood accounted for. The small-est one, Grandmoeder Geneva, stood in front of them all, her chin held high. Their attendants, with their wide, un-blinking eyes, had their arms ready in case any of them fell.

Cameron, as well as every other Arkeh:nen in earshot, bowed their heads. Sweat dripped off Cameron's nose as they waited to hear their punishment.

Grandmoeder Geneva spoke first. "Who here is hurt?"

"Basil has a broken ankle," Cameron's Moeder said, and Cameron almost cried. Broken ankles couldn't be fixed. If untreated, they could've ended up as amputa-tions. "We also have two psychics unresponsive as well as a handful of artisans who've been hurt. The numbers aren't exact. So far, no one's been killed."

Their throat tightened. Not only Avery, not only Basil, but now two psychics, an uncountable number of artisans, their own *Moeder*. The Grandmoeders shouldn't have wasted their precious energy banishing them. A true Arkeh:nen would've climbed up to the surface and never returned again.

Their Moeder motioned for them to stand, a light tap on their back. "Tell them what you just told me."

"I can't."

"You must. Think about Avery."

"Where is she?" Grandmoeder Nai asked. "Don't tell me she's responsible for this."

In a cowardly act to save themselves, Cameron almost blamed Avery for their own actions, but they couldn't do that to her. Not now. "I went into the caves with her."

The crowd disapproved with outcry.

"You brought her into the *caves*?" Grandmoeder Nai asked. "How *dare* you. How could you think of bringing her there?"

"I'm sorry."

"She who can't see in the dark, who has never been in our systems before, you thought she could handle that?"

Cameron covered their head. When would this end? When would they be banished? When would they be reunited with Avery again? That's all they wanted, was her.

"We might want to take in Cameron's side of the story before we chastise them on something that may or may not have been their fault," Grandmoeder Geneva said.

"You can't always take their side just because they're your grandchild," Grandmoeder Nai snapped. "Take responsibility for their actions."

"No!" Cameron blurted out. "Please, don't take responsibility for what I've done. This was my fault. I told her to go. I thought bad things. I'm sorry."

Grandmoeder Geneva didn't break eye contact with them. "I think of every Arkeh:nen as my child. I don't choose favorites. I just want answers that'll help move Arkeh:na forwards. Without Cameron's side of the story, we are at a standstill, and your own grandson's injuries will be based on nothing."

At this, Grandmoeder Nai finally looked down at her grandson struggling to sit up with Maywood's help. Her face softened a touch.

"Now, Cameron, tell us what happened."

Cameron slowed down their breathing. It only made them cough. "I was showing her the sights and sounds of the caves. I brought her to the oak tree thinking she'd love it, and she did. Then we...we kissed...and I asked her to stay forever, and then the walls collapsed." They pointed to the area on their *kaart*. They couldn't stop their finger from shaking. "We weren't doing anything wrong. We were just standing and hugging and then…"

"And the walls just collapsed here," their Moeder said, defending them.

"Then it couldn't have been from you alone," Grandmoeder Geneva said. "Unless you bear the forces of an earthquake, it seems that this was just an unfortunate situation brought onto us by fate."

"A fate that they created," Grandmoeder Nai reminded them.

"But Avery," Cameron said. "Grandmoeder Geneva, Avery's trapped. She could be underneath rubble or buried or worse. I don't know, but I—I-I—" They coughed, spit and snot jumping off of their face. When they opened their eyes, they saw a harsh amount of blood mixed in with their phlegm.

Their Moeder's hand touched the middle of their back.

"Can you show us where she is now?" Grandmoeder Geneva asked.

Conflicting answers arose in their heart. "No, not you. Please. It's too far away. Let me go."

"I'll go," their Moeder said. "They can stay here and rest. May I take a few others?"

"…I'll go," an excavator said from the back of the crowd. When Grandmoeder Geneva surveyed the crowd with a wordless gaze, she pulled in a few others to volunteer.

"Wait," Cameron said. "Please, take me with you. I know exactly where she is. It's my fault fate has done this to her. Let me be the one to help her, *please.*"

Their Moeder looked over their bruises. "I don't want you getting hurt."

"I won't!"

"Are you feeling better?"

They held back a cough, their esophagus burning with lies. "Yeah."

"Then get your things and lead the way."

Chapter 14: Runaway

Avery always wondered what passing out felt like. She'd seen movies where people lost consciousness, and whenever she presented in class, she dreaded the light-headedness that foreshadowed the tumble. She didn't even remember it happening, but when she awoke, she couldn't breathe, and the memories of the cave-in buried her.

She was still alive—she had to count her blessings—but she couldn't see anything. A pile of dirt was crushing her chest. Whenever she took a slight breath, the rocks shifted, threatening to entomb her.

Minutes passed. Why had Cameron left her? Surely she'd said everything right, so why hadn't they returned? Why hadn't they stayed to comfort her in a situation so dire?

Another wave of tearful panic suffocated her. She started breathing more and more until she was wheezing on the dusty air. When she felt something light touch her cheek, she imagined a long-legged spider and thrashed to keep it from entering her mouth.

Then she heard it: footsteps. Savior footsteps, stranger footsteps. Nonetheless, she screamed to be heard. "Help!"

The person carried the daintiest light source with them that barely illuminated the rocks around them. Avery had imagined the rocks as boulders incapable of moving, but it turned out to be a soft mountain of pebbles fused together to create a wall.

The person spoke in Arkeh:nen and loomed over her.

It was Cameron's Moeder. Her lantern shone against the curve of her chin, depicting her as a bodiless ghost. She had a scary head injury that was bleeding into her eye socket. Even though she was hurt, she kept her face calculated and emotionless.

When she fondled Avery's cheek, Avery welled up. She thought she'd never feel the touch of another person again. "I can't move. I can't—I'm scared."

"*Can you feel your legs?*" she asked in Arkeh:nen.

"*No. A little. They're…*" She couldn't remember the word for "numb," so she said, "*It hurts.*"

Checking the stability of the wall, Cameron's Moeder tried to move it only for pieces of it to fall on Avery's face.

Cameron's Moeder took in the gravity of the situation with a bit lip, then shouted something at the rocks. At first, Avery thought she was trying to communicate with the dirt, but then she heard muffled voices from the other side. They talked back and forth with Cameron's Moeder, and she nodded to herself and rubbed Avery's cheek like a mother would. Then she put her arms around Avery's armpits.

"Wait—"

Pain radiated down her lower back. Her upper half pulled away from the wreckage while her legs refused to move. Someone grabbed her boot from the other side and pushed, sending a tidal wave of rocks over her. Before she could warn them to stop, she started coming loose like a tooth around decaying gums.

Lantern light shone through the wall. Excavators cut her out with shovels and pickaxes, covering her with pebbles, and through the hole, exerting themselves the hardest, was Cameron. They had dirt caked underneath their fingernails and scratches on their face, but they smiled as their hand touched hers.

She tore away from them. Tears fell down her own dirt-covered cheeks. Even though she'd been freed, the suffocating feelings stayed inside of her, growing like a forest fire. "Why did you leave me alone? Why didn't you tell me you were leaving? You left almost immediately and I didn't know what happened to you!"

Cameron fell back. "The Community...I couldn't dig you out myself."

"But you knew I was scared! You knew I didn't want to be here alone."

"But...the Community—"

"Oh, enough with the Community already!"

Cameron's face cracked with affliction.

"I don't want to hear about them right now. I almost died, and you left me. You left me for them."

"Well, of course I did."

Avery choked. Why was she arguing with them? Of course that's what they thought. They'd never change their opinion on something so ingrained into them.

So she ran. She stumbled around the Moeder who'd consoled her and ignored the people who'd dug her out. Anger overtook reason. Her brains had been crushed and her feelings were bleeding into her veins, driving her away from her rescuers.

The niche the tree had grown in for so many years had been buried. The oak was uprooted, now halfway out of the ground, creating a bridge to the surface.

Before any of them stopped her, before she had a moment to rethink herself, she climbed across the dead tree and broke for the night world above.

A coating of frost slipped her down the hill outside the cave. Every stump and outcrop knocked the wind out of her and filled her mouth with ice cold dirt.

She rolled halfway down the grass and ended up on her back, staring up at the starry night sky. The pain that'd drove her away throbbed into her hip, reminding her of her fragileness.

She breathed on puffs of frozen air. Snowflakes melted on her cheeks. Through the evergreen pine, some faraway planet twinkled like a star.

With her back wet with snow, she flipped to her side and heaved herself up. Her guilt kept her warm as she limped back home.

Sometimes, she thought her dogs were human. When she trudged through the bushes and hit the driveway, they sprung up as one expected of two huskies. They barked and tugged on their leashes to reach her, but when they saw her disheveled nature, they drew back in whimpers.

Too hurt to indulge in their energy, she pet each of them once and forced herself up the steps.

The door thrust open before she touched the handle. Her father, breath caught in his throat, puffed out his chest and barred her from entering.

Avery looked up at him, his glasses skewed, and he looked at her, her sweater torn and face streaked with tears.

The first sniffle cascaded into a rainfall of tears. She'd saved face in front of Cameron's Moeder and in the presence of the forest, but with him, she couldn't hold back. Falling against him, she clung to his chest and sobbed.

He doubled over her and hugged back. "Juniper, it's her. Oh, Avery, baby, what happened to you? Are you okay?"

Her mother was already at the door. She threw her cane against the wall, spooking the dogs, and collapsed into her family. She hid her tears better than her husband.

Avery bit her cheek. Her mother's embrace felt more crushing than rocks.

"W-were you still on line with the police?" her father asked.

Her mother held Avery tighter, hurting her, loving her, in ways she'd never felt before. Not even when she'd fallen into the crevasse a year ago had her mother acted this way.

Her father forced himself away and picked up the phone, which had also been thrown due to Avery's arrival. "Yes, hello. It's Ethan. She just came home. She's okay. She's scraped and bruised—Avery, what happened?"

"A cave-in. I got trapped. I couldn't get out."

Her father retold the story to the person on the phone, but what did that matter? The police would come regardless to hear the story from her firsthand. When that happened, they'd find out about her secrets and question her about questions she didn't want to answer. Right now, all she wanted was her bed, her headphones, and her music set to max.

Her mother held her at arm's reach. "Are you hurt?"

"My legs hurt. My lower half got buried."

Her mother hobbled into the kitchen. Avery, suddenly alone despite everyone talking about her, picked up her mother's cane and walked it over to her.

"Get off your legs," her mother said. "Sit down in the living room. Ethan, get some blankets. She's freezing. Get the heated one."

Her mother and father coddled her with care. Blankets, pillows, dinner from that night, hot chocolate. She drank it scalding to shock her back awake.

"So you feel okay?" her father asked, sitting beside her on the couch.

"Yeah, I just hurt all over. I'm sorry for making you worry. I lost my bag."

"I don't care about your bag," her mother said. "Avery, we thought you got kidnapped or..." She stopped herself before her mind went someplace dark. "No more exploring the forest, okay? You're done."

As much as she wanted to argue that the forest was her safe place, she found herself nodding. "Okay."

Then her mother hugged her once more, and that somehow made Avery cry more.

With her stomach full and body warm, she walked up to her room with her mother's help. Her mother even allowed something she'd never allowed since getting them: She let Pumpkin and Oreo upstairs on the carpet. It could've been because someone had driven up the driveway with their lights on—a police car—and her father motioned the dogs upstairs. Pumpkin and Oreo didn't complain. Neither did Avery.

The dogs cuddled around her bed as her mother propped up her legs with pillows. Aside from bruising, they looked fine, but her mother didn't take her eyes off the wounded skin.

"I'm sorry," Avery repeated. "I wasn't thinking."

"Don't apologize. I'm sure you did everything you could."

"I don't think I did."

The front door opened to a stern-sounding man asking her father questions.

Avery buried her face in Pumpkin's fur.

"It's okay," her mother said. "You're not in trouble."

"I feel like I am. I shouldn't have gone as far as I did. I screwed up."

"Don't worry about that right now." She pushed back her hair. "No more woods, okay? No more woods for a while."

"I know." She wiped her frozen nose on Pumpkin and waited until the front door closed. She wondered if the session with the officer was over or if her father had politely taken the conversation outside. "Mom, can I ask you a question?"

"No, your Forest Ban isn't over yet. It just started."

She almost smiled, but her feelings reconsidered that. "With Cameron, do you think...?"

What was she going to ask? What did her mother need to know about them, someone who she didn't even like in the first place? Even after running away from them—*yelling* at them—they still wouldn't leave her mind.

"What about her? Did she have something to do with this?"

"No," Avery lied. "I was going to meet with them, but the cave-in stopped that from happening." She covered her face completely in Pumpkin's fur. "Do you like them? Even if they're strange, even if they believe in certain things, is it okay for me to be with them?"

"Well, I've never met this person before. Why do you ask?"

"Because I like them, but sometimes what they believe in and how they act is strange to me. Sometimes I don't get it, and it makes me frustrated. Today, I think I...I said something mean to them."

"Well, when you're feeling better, you can text her and apologize. If it's really bad, call her."

Avery sighed. She'd never convince her that Cameron didn't have access to a phone and that she wouldn't be seeing them at school in a few days.

Her father opened the front door. "Jun, can you come down here for a second?"

Her mother sat up. "I'll be right back, okay? I'll be right outside. And these two can stay up here tonight, but *just* for tonight, okay?"

"Okay. Thank you."

Once her mother left, Avery stared up vacantly at the ceiling. She could still smell the musty cave on her hands. So badly had she wanted to tell her mother everything right there, about the cave people living underneath the mountains, about Cameron, about what they shared.

Distraught with grief, she beckoned Oreo onto her lap and cried into his black and white fur.

Chapter 15: Restless

A baby was born on the second layer of the southern dens. They heard it was a girl and that she was very healthy despite the midwife's concerns. Her Moeder was a psychic, so the birth made the Community very happy for the potential psychic in the making.

Basil and Maywood visited Cameron every day. First three times a day, then twice, then once in the morning. Claire did, too, and so did their neighbors. Claire brought them honey, their neighbors, a basket of apples. Maywood brought them cooked squirrel and fresh drinking water. When Cameron wouldn't eat, Basil gave them some of his *gemmes*, trying anything to get them out of bed. Cameron returned everything they could until their growling stomach hurt.

"Please," Maywood said, handing them a bucket of water. "At least wash your face."

For her, they did, but they didn't know why. They weren't going out to see anyone. They didn't want to. They didn't deserve to.

"Oh, enough with the Community already!"

Was it wrong for them to always put their family over themselves? Were they always like that, enough so that Avery had gotten fed up with them and their beliefs?

They hid themselves underneath their pelt.

"Oh, enough with the Community already!"

Ever since she left, they'd been holding onto her *fone*. Basil had told them not to open it too often or else the "battery" would run out. They didn't—they didn't want to lose their sight. They simply held onto it, hoping for it to vibrate and magically connect them to Avery. They wanted one word from her, just one. Anything to spark up a conversation with her.

It never rang.

Chapter 16: New Year

She'd planned on spending her birthday with them. She'd planned on having two Christmas parties, one with her family around their fake tree and honeyed ham, one with Cameron, celebrating whatever harvest or winter solstice they believed in. Maybe they didn't believe in anything and continued on into the new year without flair.

She never got to find out.

December went by like the weather: slow, and cold. Four inches coated the balconies at any given time. Storms cancelled half of her father's work, her mother didn't get called into the office, and school lost almost all of its Fridays to snow. Through November into December, Avery ghosted through her humdrum life with a snowed-in head.

Nothing about her life made sense after the cave-in. She didn't feel depressed—she didn't talk or smile as much, but she never talked or smiled much before Arkeh:na. She had nothing to be sad about, anyway; with Christmas coming into view, all she had to look forward to was spending time with her family.

A week before Christmas break and normalcy soaked back into her. She kept her head down at her locker. She received average marks in English and above-average ones in science. Nobody asked how her Thanksgiving went, nobody asked about her caving adventures. The shortened school week carried on without her speaking a word to anyone.

Skipping class was easy when nobody wanted to teach in the first place. Every student and teacher had their eyes on the windows, waiting for that one flake of snow. Because of this, Avery got to sneak her lunch bag to the library. With the amount of students at her school, nobody would go looking for one missing girl during study hall. She'd left her phone in Arkeh:na, anyway, so she had nothing to distract herself with.

Their library resided on the first floor. It had the least amount of renovations done to it compared to the whole building. It still retained its creaky floors and paling wallpaper from the early 1900s. Before she took up hiking, she'd spent several long, lonely years in this expansive room. She knew its layout almost as well as her hiking trails.

Finding her favorite shelf in the library—the comic book section—Avery picked up a random title and began reading. She looked at the pictures more than anything, partly due to her feelings, partly due to a class being held in the library's recreational room. Its doors were closed, but she could still hear the thrum of a distracting lecture.

When the bell rang, students gathered their bags and filed out of the double doors.

She hid her face in her comic. Cameron would definitely like comics. Whenever she returned, she had to bring back a couple for them. They could read them together underneath a firebug lantern, sharing a bowl of warm porridge.

Someone came up behind her, their eyes digging into her back. She waited it out, hoping they'd leave, but they didn't. Sighing, she peeked behind her to see who was upset with her now.

Bridget Rodríguez stared at her with her backpack halfway off of her shoulder, her books slipping out of her hands. She had her hair down, a hairstyle she'd once told Avery she wasn't confident in, and had on a white button down she'd never seen her in before. It showed off the cross around her neck.

Avery waited for somebody to speak first. Bridget examined the books on her left. She tucked her gelled hair around her ears. She had on that perfume she'd worn the day Avery lost her. Tropical fruit.

Avery shoved the comic back onto the shelf and walked passed her. Her legs brought her to the tall windows showcasing the track field outside. She settled down in one of the library bean bags and didn't breathe until all the beads in the bag shifted to her weight.

Second period of lunch started. Students turned on the computers. The librarian went to fix herself some coffee.

Silent tears fell from Avery's face as she watched a flock of geese land on the field. Too stubborn to fly south, they searched the snowy grounds for food. After thirty minutes of pecking, one flew away, and the rest followed behind it as hungry stragglers.

She told herself she was okay throughout Christmas break.

Her father picked up her grandparents that Monday and drove them up the hill for a week-long sleepover. He'd pressured them to close down the shop to spend the week with them, something they almost got into a fight about. When Avery teared up at the sound of their arguing, they folded and slept upstairs in the spare bedroom.

She didn't know if that made her feel better. Now she needed to maneuver around four observant family members instead of two. Questions about her health and mood dogged her around the house, and she had to keep up with the lies while digging herself a deeper hole.

Christmas dinner worked out in her favor. Sitting around the table, nobody wanted to drop their forks and delve into Avery's problems when conversations about the weather and mountains proved to be less dispiriting.

"How much longer are you gonna be out in those mountains?" her grandmother asked from across the table. "Your wife needs someone around the house to babysit this one, since she's still under house arrest."

"I'm happy with him working and earning money for the family," her mother said.

"The plan's set to be done around next summer," her father said. "Avery, I was thinking we can go hiking together before then...in some newer parts of the forest. Do you want to go to Black River and hike up its riverbed?"

"No caves to get lost in there," her grandfather said. "Hey, Avery, when did you get that necklace? It's pretty."

Avery stopped twirling Cameron's necklace around her finger. Normally, she'd hide it inside of her shirt, but it kept popping out, giving her hands something to play with.

"It *is* pretty," her grandmother added.

"A good friend of mine gave it to me."

"Was it that witch friend of yours?"

She dragged her fork through her mashed potatoes.

"I don't think..." her father started, then restarted with, "You know, Ash, I wanted to ask you something about the business. I was thinking you take off next week for your health..."

Avery slumped into her hand. Her mind told her to listen to the conversation, but she couldn't. What she had with Cameron had been a fallen tree in her trail, yet instead of picking a new way to walk, she'd been sitting in the middle of the wet dirt, waiting for someone to redirect her.

She sighed so as not to provoke a reaction from her family and lifted her droopy head to watch the snow fall.

A pair of brown eyes locked onto hers. Through the frost-covered windows, Basil was somehow staring back at her. He hung from the balcony like a criminal peering through jail bars, his fingerless gloves latched onto the balusters.

After catching her eyes, he let go and disappeared. By the sound of his fall, it sounded like he landed on his back.

Avery sprung up from her chair. "I have to go."

"Where?" her father asked.

"Uh, outside. I heard Pumpkin...fussing."

"Don't bring them in," her mother said. "When Pumpkin sees the turkey, there'll be no stopping her."

"I won't," she said, and sped-walked to the garage.

Pumpkin and Oreo were gone, but their long leashes were wrapped around the open garage door.

She plodded around the side of the house, following their trail. Had she really seen him? While she couldn't let her parents find a boy creeping around their home, she couldn't let them see her walking through the snow, calling out a type of spice to see if it answered back.

Pumpkin and Oreo had found Basil first. He stood casually beneath their laundry room windows, petting the two of them. He wore a fur jacket, thick and brown like a bear pelt, with a rabbit-fur hood framing his face and black gloves. He brought a traveling pack with him along with Avery's backpack. She'd lied about misplacing her bag and phone, so her parents had bought her new ones for Christmas, but her sketchbook, her hat, her pins...

"Hey," he greeted, and tossed her her backpack.

She grabbed it awkwardly and opened it, revealing her untouched sketchbook and hat, everything but her phone.

"After the cave-in, none of the scavengers wanted to bring this back," Basil said. *"Cameron kept sleeping with it. I thought it'd be healthier if I returned it."*

She almost missed half of his words. It'd been so long since she'd spoken the language. *"I thought you weren't allowed outside. You're not a scavenger."*

Basil scratched Pumpkin's chin. *"It's easy to leave. It's harder to stay away."*

Avery looked over his odd stance. As he pet her dogs, he had one foot off the ground like a flamingo. Strange bandages were wrapped around his ankle.

Once he noticed her staring, he tugged down his pant cuff.

"Are you okay?"

"Yeah," he said. *"I left your phone with Cameron. It's not expensive, right?"*

She didn't know if he was being sarcastic, but with his curious expression, she said, *"It's okay. How're they doing?"*

He looked away. *"They told me not to tell you."*

"Tell me."

She hadn't meant to sound so assertive, but Basil blinked back before saying, *"They don't leave their den anymore. Only to bathe and eat, but it's infrequent. And they've stopped talking to the Community. A baby was born a few weeks ago and they still haven't gone to see it. I've never seen them like this before. Do you hate them?"*

"No," she said instantly. *"Never. I don't know what's wrong with me. I've been feeling scared and...wrong. I haven't felt like this since I met Cameron. Please tell them I'll come back soon. I just need to fix something inside me, and I think I have to be alone to do that."*

"Alright," he said, verbally unsatisfied with her reasoning. *"Hopefully that'll make both you and them happy."* He looked up to the balcony he'd just jumped from. *"Today's a holiday, right?"*

"Yeah. We call it Christmas."

"Was that your family up there? Are you celebrating it with them?"

She nodded.

"They look like you. That must be nice."

She didn't know what to say. She knew he was still looking for his father. She'd told him she'd look, but there was no real way she could find him without taking a blood sample from Basil and every man who looked like him in the county. In her mind, he knew that, and he still kept looking.

She checked to make sure none of her family members were spying on her. *"Do you want to come in?"*

He snorted. *"I once entered an Autrean house. I saw a black cat on the windowsill and wanted to pet it. The old woman living there screamed when she saw me and grabbed her gun."*

"Oh, dear. Were you hurt? I don't think people can shoot you if you break into their property in New York."

"New York," he said fondly. *"That's what this place is called, isn't it? Isn't that weird? I've lived here all my life, yet I don't know anything about it. Don't they say something to one another on this day? Something like Happy...Merry..."*

"Merry Christmas."

He pulled off his hood. *"Merry Christmas. I hope you get to fix whatever's broken inside of you today, if it's able to be fixed at all. I know it's hard to move forwards when you're busy picking up the broken pieces left behind."*

She went to wish him an equally healing Christmas, but a snowflake caught in her throat. Sniffling, she dropped her head and choked on her tears. She'd gone most of the holiday keeping it together. She was so proud of herself for making it this far.

Breaking the distance between them, Basil took Avery in his arms and held her until she felt warm.

Chapter 17: Cameron's Reading

Cameron lay in bed, staring at Avery's phone, holding their stomach in pain. They would've blamed the throbbing on hunger—they hadn't eaten all day—but they knew why they felt so awful.

Every time they closed their eyes, they saw Avery yelling at them for their misdoings. They'd tried to explain themselves, but it hadn't been enough. Nothing could ever be enough for her.

They didn't understand. Avery knew about their condition—she called it "asthma"—so she knew they couldn't have dug her out by themselves. They'd done what they thought was best by calling the Community for help. And the whole ordeal with the Grandmoeders didn't help at all. It felt like a part of them was still buried in that *tunnle* and they hadn't the strength to call out for help.

Maybe they should've comforted her first, or maybe they should've told her they were going to get help. Maybe, maybe, maybe. The word haunted them and their spur-of-the-moment decisions.

A burning feeling settled in their throat. Choking, they reached for the bucket they'd borrowed from their neighbors and coughed hard into it. They'd hidden their ailments for days now, but they couldn't do it anymore. They had to face the truth: Their sickness was getting worse, and it was all because of what they'd done to Arkeh:na and Avery.

After spitting into the bucket, Cameron staggered to their feet and went to their *gemme* collection. None of them bothered to talk to them anymore. After several weeks of thought, Cameron had decided that they deserved a better owner.

So, taking one of their oldest *gemme* cases, Cameron packed away their most precious gemstones and brought them to Basil and Maywood.

They heard Basil from two *tunnles* away. Maywood was trying to sew him new bandages while he complained from their bed. They had a spinning wheel in their den from their Fader's time as a needleworker. It was never touched until Maywood took up her Fader's occupation.

When Cameron came in, Basil stopped arguing. "You're up."

They nodded, then looked to his swollen ankle.

He covered it. "It's getting better."

"He went outside," Maywood tattled. "When he came home, I found pine all over him, all sappy and torn."

"I was just scavenging."

"With a broken ankle! You need to take better care of yourself. I worry."

She said the last word while looking at Cameron, but Cameron couldn't look into her doting eyes for too long.

They opened their *gemme* box. "None of my *gemmes* are working for me anymore. I was wondering if you two wanted any."

"They're not working?" Maywood asked.

"No. If you could take a few off my hands, I'm sure they'll work for you. They like hard-working, loving people, so they'll like you and Basil."

Maywood touched their side, comforting them. "Cameron, I'm sorry."

"For what?"

"About Avery, about what our Grandmoeder said to you."

"What she said to you was wrong," Basil said. "She's always had it out for you and me. I'd be hard-pressed to say she likes anything."

"Don't be rude to them behind their backs," Maywood said. "Not all of us can live as long as they can. If they're able to live past fifty, they're important."

Cameron dropped four *gemmes* in Maywood's hand. "Use this one for Basil's legs and these for your Moeder. They used to help with my sadness."

Maywood pocketed them. "Cameron, I'm sure she'll come back."

"And she doesn't hate you," Basil promised. "She'll be back any day now, I know it."

"Whatever you say," Cameron said, and walked out.

They traveled around Arkeh:na like a struggling salesperson. Some neighbors took the *gemmes*, but no one wanted them in the same way no one wanted food with a bite mark in it. Yes, it'd work for its purpose, and you should've been grateful for the offer, but you'd take nearly anything else and usually felt disgusted with the overall exchange. But it was all Cameron had. What more could they do?

With nearly the same amount of *gemmes* they'd started with, Cameron climbed up to the first layer and rested at the *Centrum*. The *Centrum* had been resurrected, but the artisan corner was still destroyed. Nobody could buy new clothes or replace their cups and plates. Scavengers and strong Arkeh:nen were still digging out salvable pieces of wood.

Cameron should've been excavating with them, or going door to door to see if everyone was okay. They should've helped out weeks ago, but no. They were waiting on the girl who'd pushed them away, hoping she'd take them back the next time they disappointed her.

"Oh, enough with the Community already!"

The faintest smell of spices wafted around the *Centrum* pillars. Behind them, next to the *Rivière*, was the hole leading down to the psychics' dens. The falls created a foam of water that wafted magical herbs throughout Arkeh:na.

Cameron tapped their foot. They swore they saw the air sparkle with energy, but they knew they couldn't see such magic.

Groaning tiredly, they got up and brought their *gemmes* to the psychics' dens.

Step after step into the pits and the air cooled with misty energy. They needed to walk down a cramped *tunnle* filled with dried asters, sage, and acorns. Quilts from past Grandmoeders hung up as makeshift doors that Cameron needed to duck under. They couldn't dare touch them. Pushing them aside with such hands felt shameful.

The end of the hall opened up to a dark antechamber lined with *gemmes* on high shelves. Barron, the guard who stood watch at the main entrance, looked Cameron up and down with his arms crossed. His head reached the highest shelf. "Your Moeder's in the middle of a reading. What do you need?"

"I don't know," they said honestly. "I wanted to get rid of my *gemmes*, but no one wants them. I think they brought me here. Do you need any?"

Barron pulled out his bracelet of purple *gemmes*. "Sorry."

"Right."

"Do you want to schedule a reading?"

They didn't hate the idea of readings. They knew their influence could very well save a person's life. But when their Fader had left, they were forced to get a joint-reading with their Moeder. They were young, so they didn't remember much. All they remembered was the guilt that they'd been the one to drive their Fader away and their Moeder. She'd *cried*. It was the first time they'd seen her like that, like a person with feelings and not an all-knowing Goddess.

"You seem lost," Barron went on. "I think a reading would help. Some people"—he nodded to where the psychics worked—"come in with much more to talk about looking far better than you do. And don't say other people deserve to be seen before you."

Cameron, who'd just opened their mouth to refute him, clamped up.

Barron rolled his bracelet *gemmes* around his wrist. "Cameron, your Moeder..."

Before he said whatever he'd wanted to say, someone new entered the antechamber. Moeder Exia, Basil's and Maywood's Moeder, left the dens fixing her shawl around her bony shoulders. She would've slammed the wooden door behind her before a ringed hand lurched out from the darkness.

Cameron's Moeder left the shadows as she held open the door. "I'll take you."

They hid their box behind their back. Even though they were making eye contact with her, they didn't want to come out and ask if she wanted to see *them* or someone else, maybe Barron, maybe Moeder Exia again.

When their Moeder said nothing, Cameron lowered their head and followed her in.

"Good luck," Barron whispered.

The *tunnle* to the psychic rooms was built against the waterfall, letting a gentle flow of water sprinkle over the ceiling like rain. Cameron paused at such a rare sight. The falls in the caves burst with so much power that they couldn't near them without losing their hearing. Even water knew how to act around the psychics.

Cameron had visited their Moeder's psychic den three times. Once on accident, as they didn't know the consequences for entering without permission, the second when their Fader left, and the third from when they sliced open their skull from their first cave-in, resulting in their facial scar. Their Moeder hadn't slept as she worked tirelessly on healing her degenerate child.

Her room looked exactly the same as it did those times. Two quilts padded the ground, one for her, one for her client. Skulls and bones of dead animals made up her altars, and candles and incense had been lit to cleanse the area. The scents Cameron had smelled in the *Centrum* now dizzied them.

Their Moeder motioned for them to sit on the quilt adjacent from hers.

"I don't really need a reading," Cameron said, sitting down. "I wanted to know if any Moeders needed my *gemmes*."

"Why don't you want them?"

"I don't think they work for me anymore."

"So you think you don't deserve them?"

"Not anymore."

Their Moeder placed their box on one of her altars. A stuffed crow watched over its contents with a permanently open beak. "Why're you here?"

They laced their fingers over their lap. "I'm not sure."

"Have you heard from Avery?"

"No."

"Has anyone told you about her?"

Their heart thumped in their ears. "What happened to her? Is she sick? Is she okay?"

Their Moeder sat across from them. "She's fine," she said in monotone. "Scavengers have been keeping an eye on her. One returned her backpack to her a few days ago." She took a candle and lit it with another. Then she sat in silence for almost a minute, looking directly at Cameron.

They wished she didn't prep her sessions like this, but what did they know? They'd only heard of her practices through impressed whispers in the *ville*. But did she have to act so secretly? Didn't she already know them as her child?

She arched her back. "Close your eyes."

Cameron did as told.

The incense enhanced. The waterfall outside grew louder, as if rapping on the curtains for a fortune. They noticed the softness of the quilts and the echoes off the room. They recognized themselves as a simple, breathing person.

"Here."

Cameron opened their eyes to their Moeder holding out her signature deck. Each card had its own unique drawing and spirituality attached to it. Only skilled Moeders understood their wordless magic.

She fanned out the cards in front of them. "Pick three."

They did. Each time they picked one, their Moeder's eyebrow twitched. Cameron tried to plan out each pick, but they knew their say meant nothing. By picking these random cards, she must've known the name of their firstborn child and the date of their death or something. When they'd tried to read Avery's fortune, they couldn't even figure out what *they* were feeling, let alone her.

Once they had their three cards, their Moeder reorganized them in front of her. "This card represents your past," she explained, pointing to one card, "this one's your present, and this's your future." She picked up the past card. It was of a man balancing over the edge of a cliff. "The Fool. A reckless, selfish being."

"But I'm not selfish."

"Selfishness doesn't come from your actions, it comes from your feelings." She placed down the card. "You're getting sicker, and you haven't told me."

They tightened their core, but it caused them to cough. "I didn't want you to worry."

"You think carrying your burdens alone will somehow make things better, because you don't want your loved ones to worry. That's why you're selfish."

"But—"

151

"The cards don't care about how you feel," their Moeder stressed. "They're designed to slap you into re-thinking your actions." She picked up the next card. "The World, reversed."

Cameron winced. While they didn't know much about cards, they knew how disastrous reversed cards meant. "I don't want to do this anymore."

Their Moeder continued. "You're incomplete. You're living in a world without trees. You're stagnating without closure."

Cameron covered their ears.

"You must listen to them. They know my own child. They only want what's best for you."

"But I don't. I only want what's best for other people."

"Your future—"

"Please—"

"The Magician. It can mean willpower and a great passion. I don't believe this's your case. I believe you're heading for disaster, and you'll be facing a great deal of pain and loss very soon."

"No!"

"*Yes*. This's the person you were in the past, this's who you are now, and this's who you'll be in the future. Selfish, incomplete, and heading for disaster. Stop hiding from your problems and stop wallowing. Realize that Avery's gone because of what you did."

Cameron dropped their hands onto the quilt, their tension gone, restraints broken. Hearing it for the first time spoken so soberly, their face scrunched up in anguish, and they cried. They ugly-cried into their hands, facing their Moeder who knew best and who'd always known so.

She crawled over and held them.

"It's all my fault," they sobbed. "I'm a terrible Arkeh:nen."

"You're neither the worst nor the best. None of us are."

"But Avery's gone because of me."

"She is, and she'll return."

"No, she won't. I know she won't. Oh, Moeder, she was so angry with me when she ran away. She hates me, I know it."

"She won't hate you forever. Forever is something young people like to cling to, but you don't know what forever means. Avery will forgive you, and both of you will get to apologize to one another very soon."

"I hate it. Moeder, I hate this. I miss her so much. I want her back."

"You're in love, Cameron. There's nothing wrong with that."

At that, they cried louder. They didn't want this. They'd known since the beginning that they'd wanted Avery as a friend, maybe even a best friend, but seeing her in this light hurt beyond reason. Why did anyone fall in love if it invited so much pain into your heart?

"I know. I know falling in love is...It can be difficult, and sometimes it feels like it's not worth it. It's one thing to fall in love. It's another to stay in love and keep that love prospering, especially when both of you are changing. Me and Erik—" She corrected herself. "Your Fader and I became two very different people after I had you. He needed to leave. I needed to stay."

"But do you still love him even though he left and hurt you?"

"Do you still love Avery?"

They snuggled into her chest. They knew the answer just as well as she did.

"I know my reading for you was rather harsh. Yes, you're selfish, but you're selfish in the best possible way. And everyone's incomplete, and everyone should expect loss in life. Just prepare yourself for it. If people aren't prepared for loss, they'll lose themselves completely."

They let her words sink in. "I need to prepare?"

"Yes. You need to clear your mind and focus on what you need to do next. You need to realize what's important to you and act on it."

Cameron relished in their Moeder's hug for one more minute before they pulled away and dried their eyes. When they looked back up at her, she was faintly but noticeably smiling.

After another hug, Cameron left the psychic room in higher spirits than when they'd entered. They waved to Barron and Moeder Exia, who was spacing out near the falls. Cameron hadn't realized they'd left without their *gemme* box until they passed the *Centrum*, but they didn't care. While they loved the devotion they put into *gemmes*, something more important was guiding them now.

Trying to be as slick as possible, Cameron went back to their den and packed a bag. They packed the gifts their neighbors and friends had given them and put on an extra *gemme* necklace for good luck. After dressing into their poncho and slinging their bag onto their back, they then took hold of Avery's phone. It now radiated with more energy than any one of their *gemmes*.

Nuvu chittered at their owner's unexplained energy.

Cameron pet underneath her chin. "I'll be back soon," they promised, and left for the Main Exit *Tunnle*.

They'd seen Avery climb up these *tunnle's* steps a dozen times before, and scavengers had no problems with them. Still, they faltered at the height, unsure of what really lived in the Autre world.

They knew one thing, though: Avery lived somewhere on the surface, and if fate treated them kindly, it would lead them to her.

Coughing into the open air, they took hold of the first rung and started climbing.

Chapter 18: The Autre World

No wonder Avery wore so many layers when she came to visit. They hadn't even touched the surface yet and their teeth were chattering. When they pushed the boulder out of the way, they collapsed outside the Main Exit *Tunnle* panting out cold breath. Avery made it look easy, but the rock weighed almost as much as they did. And the coldness, it burned their fingers. They thought the rock was wet, but frost had collected on the side facing the Autre world.

Acclimating their eyes to the moonlight, Cameron bunched up their hands in their poncho and stepped outside.

The Autre night held a smell to its darkness. Crisp and clean, the smell of ice and pine. Perhaps it was the scent of the Moon, which colored the snow blue and trees black. Its cold rays of light twinkled the snow like pure *gemmes*.

They took their first step into snow and shivered with amusement. They hadn't expected it to *crunch* like that. Some parts were light, other parts sharp as rocks. They felt bad for stepping all over it. In the artisan huts, they melted this stuff down for drinking and healing water.

As they walked down the path, they turned back to see Arkeh:na's mountain growing small. The massiveness of the mountain never crossed their mind. It built itself up like an ant hill, birthing trees on its incline and helping them reach the stars. They expected more houses, at least someone wandering by. To their astonishment, not a lot of humans lived *in* the forest, just underneath it.

They looked behind them again to see how far they'd gotten.

They couldn't see the mountain.

They stopped. They couldn't see the mountain. They hadn't been paying attention to where they were walking, and now they were lost. Never in the past five years had they gotten lost.

They traced their *kaart* scars and kept going. They'd find Avery soon enough. How many people could live in New York? They'd seen pictures of her home. Finding a log cabin in the woods would be easy.

After traveling around trees and icy patches of snow, they came across a path made of hard stone. They almost crossed it before remembering what Basil had told them about "streets." Taking his advice, they checked both ways and didn't see or hear any "cars." Only crickets whistling their songs.

They followed a faded line painted on the edge of the street. They had yet to see any houses or dens. The thought of Avery traveling so long for their sake astounded them.

A low rumbling revved up behind them. They stepped out of the way, thinking it a low cave-in, but two bright, burning lights blinded them with bestial screams.

Cameron rolled into the snowbank to keep from getting eaten. What on Earth was it? Their eyes hurt too much to take it in. They were left to listen to it bare its mechanical teeth at them. When it drove off, the wind sliced off its wheels in a snarl and screeched like a banshee grieving for her lost child.

Cameron clutched their pounding chest and stumbled down the road opposite of the "car." They swore they saw a pair of human eyes trapped within the contraption, but they didn't dwell on that nightmare image for long.

Ten minutes later and they braced themselves on a tree to wheeze. The air was beginning to hurt their throat and numb their feet. This never happened in Arkeh:na, as it kept a modest temperature year round. How did Autreans survive this weather outside of dens?

They looked up. Through the trees, peeking out like curious cat eyes, the Autrean homes came out of hiding.

Cameron stepped onto a wider road. This one had balls of light affixed to branchless trees. Ghostly dogs howled into the night as cars revved down distant roads.

They took out Avery's phone. Things like footprints or breathing weren't enough to announce your presence here. For Autreans, you needed light in order to be seen.

So they entered the town of Foxfield. Its name rang true: It had fields as long as *tunnles* where foxes could safely live. And it smelled like animals, and not in a cooked meat kind of way. They smelled poop and fur and the living spaces of hefty work animals. One even crossed the street with them, its large eyes glowing yellow.

Wondering what types of critters lived with modern humans, Cameron crept up to a red house surrounded by a wooden fence. They stuck their head through an opened window.

Something as large as a car and equally formidable pressed up against their cheek. It sniffed them with teeth, grazing their skin, before pulling back and chuffing. It had a snout as big as Cameron's head with eyes as black as a bear's. It didn't move, but its breathing came from deep within its spotted stomach.

Cameron knew them vaguely as "cows."

They lowered the phone and slowly backed away, never taking their eyes off the beast. Its pupil-less eyes faded back into the darkness.

They continued on. Ten houses down that road, six up that hill. Just outside the cow's house lived hundreds, maybe even thousands of homes. On instinct, they kept tracing their *kaart* for direction, but they wouldn't find it here. Every house had some element of Avery's home: doors, windows, garages. Which one did she live in?

They looked down at the phone. Avery had explained to them that you needed to press buttons to call someone. She'd demonstrated it months ago, but the calls never "went through" because they were in a cave. Cameron had nodded like they understood what that meant.

They started pressing buttons.

The screen shut off, reflecting their confused face back at them.

Of course. If they didn't crack the world in half come March of next year, they'd be so impressed with their luck.

They kept walking, on and on, down the unwinding streets. The snow had molded dirty mountains around the roads that they needed to keep climbing over. Sometimes the lights atop the branchless trees flickered when they neared and startled them.

Some Autreans even walked past. Usually, when two Arkeh:nen walked past one another in *tunnles*, they'd say "hello" or affectionately touch one another's hands. The

Autreans did neither. Most of them looked at Cameron with distasteful looks.

Cameron patted down their hair. The Autreans looked so pretty and well kept. Their clothes didn't have holes in them and their faces were scarless. They'd always thought Avery looked one-of-a-kind, but seeing other Autreans en masse, they began thinking that they were the strange one.

At the end of one street, Cameron passed a group of people their own age. One of the girls stopped like they recognized them. She looked a little like Avery with her dark hair and skin, so they explained to her that they were looking for a girl named Avery and that they needed to find her house so that they could apologize to her for leaving her behind during a cave-in.

The girl and her group of friends chuckled nervously and walked away, leaving Cameron underneath a flickering light.

Head down, Cameron sped up the closest hill near an empty farm. They now understood why Avery had closed herself off when they first met. Instead of wanting to get to know you, Autreans found ways of hating you before anything else. At least in Arkeh:na, people pretended to like you and never said anything about it. You had to see them the next day, after all.

They passed something that looked like a log cabin, but painted apples with unnerving smiles glared at them and sent them up the mountain.

They sneezed into the open air. How did Avery walk all this way multiple times a week? How did Basil *enjoy* this, going out without permission and exploring such unforgiving lands? Arkeh:na had nothing akin to these hills—

their ancestors would've put up ladders or rope for smoother travels. This road stretched on for nearly a mile with only a metal railing to hold on to. It burned to the touch.

But then finally, after breathing in the freezing air, after getting coated in ice, Cameron found something. The cabin looked almost identical to the one on Avery's phone, but the sizing looked wrong. It felt too flamboyant and spacious for her. Still, they were freezing, tired, and angry at themselves that they'd even left in the first place. If anything, they'd hide beneath this cabin's many roofs, which, angled in the way they were, had been built to keep snow from piling up on top of them. Autreans had thought of everything except how to walk up and down icy streets during winter.

The house had multiple doors and multiple door-sized windows. Picking one at random, Cameron walked up its slippery steps and tried opening it.

It was locked. Why did Autreans lock their doors?

They didn't know what they'd done wrong, but the house exploded with commotion. Lights zapped on. Dogs barked. Before they could run away, someone unlocked the door.

Avery's Fader, a tall, black Fader with glasses, held back Avery's two dogs by their collars. He didn't look angry, but he didn't look happy. He looked ready to sic these animals on them for trespassing. *"Who...need...you... you?"*

Cameron understood half of his words. *"Avery, I think she live here. She's a friend, my—"*

The Fader turned around and called out Avery's name, followed by a question. While they waited, Cameron stared at the dogs' wolf-like muzzles. They were "Oreo" and "Pumpkin." Avery said they were sweet and tempered. Did she know what "sweet" and "tempered" meant?

Another dark-skinned Autrean—Avery's Moeder—looked around the Fader's broad shoulder, her eyebrow cocked with suspicion.

She made room for her daughter, who plowed through her own Moeder and Fader to see Cameron cowering on her doorstep.

"Cameron?" Avery asked. "What're you doing here?"

Chapter 19: Sleepover

"Avery," Cameron said, relieved. *"You're really here."*

She didn't believe that. As soon as she saw them standing there, she thought she was still half-asleep. She hadn't showered yet. She was wearing a throw-away band t-shirt from sixth grade. How much worse could this nightmare have gotten? She hadn't even prepped her parents on meeting Cameron yet, someone they'd not only hate, but not understand. How would she explain this to them?

Their expressions said it all: her father, thunderstruck as he held open the door; her mother, totally lost and a little insulted by a late-night guest.

Cameron's skinny legs trembled. *"I-I've been searching for you f-for hours. Why do you live so far away?"*

Her parents looked at her to see if they needed to call the police. She called them off, then yelled at her dogs to go to their beds in the living room. It took two warnings before they finally listened. Their eyes never left Cameron.

Knowing they weren't going to get bitten, Cameron entered their home without permission.

Avery, as well as her parents, stepped back. "What're you doing here?"

They frowned at her use of English. She knew they didn't like speaking it, but she had no choice. "I, uh, leave, to you."

"Why? I thought you weren't allowed to leave if you weren't a—" She wanted to say "scavenger," but she didn't want her parents to question the odd work profession.

"My Moeder...say this, I think, in a reading. I go to you." They acknowledged her parents with a bow. *"Is this your Moeder and Fader? They look so much like you."*

"Is this a friend from school?" her father asked.

"Uh, yeah," she said. "In my science class...and lunch period. They—" She winced. They wouldn't get it. They wouldn't get any of this. Why was Cameron here? Did they seriously travel all this way for her?

She chose the gender that'd make them the happiest. "This's Cameron. She'd called me beforehand saying she wanted to come over. I forgot to tell you."

"Oh." Her mother checked the grandfather clock behind her. "It's...so late, though. It's almost ten."

"Uh, yeah. She lives far away. I didn't think she was going to walk here. That's why she's so dirty."

"She must be freezing," her father said, and Avery leapt at the chance. She just needed to get Cameron away from them.

"Right," she said, and took Cameron's sleeve. "Look at her. She's shivering. Let me, uh, draw a bath for them to warm them up."

"Does she need anything for those scrapes?" her father asked.

"They're fine!" she almost shouted, and pushed Cameron up the stairs.

"I'm not a girl," Cameron reminded her.

"*I know, just play along,*" she whispered, and locked them inside of her upstairs bathroom.

Cameron shook off her tight hand. "*Why're you acting so strange?*"

"*Me, acting strange? What about you? What're you doing here?*"

"*I was worried. You never came back. I thought something might've happened to you. Are you okay?*"

"*Yes, but...*" She gagged at their swollen knees. "*What happened?*"

"*A car came close to me, so I ducked into the snow to avoid it. I walked everywhere trying to find your house.*"

"*You shouldn't have left in the first place. It's too dangerous here.*" She squatted down to the tub and drew their bath. "*You can wash up here, but do it quick.*"

Cameron leaned over her. "*This's the thing you explained to me, right? A bathtub?*"

"*Yeah.*"

"*Is this yours?*"

"*Yeah.*" She tested the water's temperature on her pinkie.

A light hand touched the nape of her neck. "*Hey.*"

She shivered.

'Apologize,' her brain begged. '*Tell them you're sorry, that you didn't mean the hurtful things you said. Say anything to keep their hands on you.*'

Just a month without them and she was already thinking bad thoughts. What made it worse was that she wanted it. She wanted more of them. She would've apologized for everything she'd ever done if it meant they'd keep touching her.

They massaged her neck. *"I'm sorry I left you back in the* tunnle. *I should've stayed with you so you weren't alone. I wasn't thinking. I'm sorry."*

'Apologize.'

'Apologize already.'

'Kiss them and apologize.'

She got up. She opened the medicine cabinet to search for nothing in particular. Her words spiraled into the sink. *"It's fine. The water should be fine now. Take a bath, wash up. I'll be outside."*

Cameron wiggled out of their poncho, revealing their skin-tight bodysuit that hugged every inch of their body.

Avery ran out of the bathroom and sat on the corner of her bed, her hands folded around her mouth. Had Arkeh:nen always been so open like that, or was Cameron thinking too much into their relationship?

Their relationship. What did that mean? She'd just run away from them. Again. That's all she knew how to do, to save herself.

—◇—

A while later, Cameron came out wearing just their poncho and shorts. They'd scrubbed off a layer of dirt from their skin. Their curly hair now reached past their shoulders in soaking locks.

"You shouldn't put on the same thing after you shower," Avery said, *"but I guess I didn't leave you with anything to change into."*

"Do you have anything I can wear?"

"I think." She pulled out a turtleneck and a pair of pajama bottoms from her drawers. She pushed down the t-

shirts with animated characters on them. As they showered, she'd cleansed her room of embarrassing items and stuffed them in her closet. *"These should be good."*

Cameron began undressing at her bedside.

Avery choked and turned around. She felt lightheaded with how many ups and downs they were dragging her through. Was she truly awake right now?

"You're acting so jumpy," Cameron said. *"What's wrong?"*

"I didn't expect you, so I'm trying to keep it cool so my parents don't freak out."

They sat on her bed. *"Why do you say that like it's a bad thing?"*

"It's not. You don't know my parents. I don't think they'll like you."

"I just met them. How do they not like me?"

"Because they don't like strange things. They like order and things they understand."

"So you think I'm strange?"

"Of course not, but to them, yes." She checked downstairs. Of course they'd think them strange. Her mother thought so badly about magic people, and her father was so...*normal*. She couldn't let them break someone so precious to her.

Her father appeared by the staircase. "Avery, how long is your friend staying over again? Is she hungry?"

Avery translated the question to Cameron, but she didn't receive an answer. Through the moonlight, they found them *scowling* at her, their upper lip curled like she'd offended them.

"What?"

"I'm strange?" they asked, defensive. "Why would you say that?"

"I didn't. I said my parents will think you're strange."

"But that doesn't make a difference."

"What're you getting on about?"

"Avery?"

"Uh, sure, Dad," she called down.

"You know I have problems with my image. All my life I thought I was weird because I couldn't do magic readings like my Moeder. Why would you reinforce it?"

"I wasn't—"

"But you just did!"

Avery glanced over the railing. "Okay," she whispered. "I'm sorry. I'm not thinking straight right now. I have a lot on my mind."

"About what? You're not telling me anything."

"You wouldn't understand, and I don't want to talk about it right now. It'll only make me sadder."

"But maybe talking about it would—"

"Can you please just drop it?"

That finally got Cameron to quit. "This isn't you," they muttered. "This isn't like you."

They shared the rest of last night's macaroni and cheese in silence. Avery drank hot chocolate while Cameron figured out how to eat Autrean food. Apparently, they'd never eaten cheese before.

"It tastes bad," they'd told her.

"So don't eat it."

As the clock chimed ten, Avery yawned and felt up her pillow for rest. Cameron, working on Arkeh:nen time, kept getting up and exploring her room. They inspected her closet and fireplace, then got lost in the bathroom and played with the faucet.

She didn't know why she wouldn't allow herself to enjoy this rare moment with them, but something inside of her told her to keep quiet. In the right circumstances, having a sleepover with them would've been a dream. Now she couldn't wait to wake up to an empty bedroom.

At eleven, she thought she heard her parents go to bed, so she covered her lower half with her blankets. *"I'm going to bed."*

Cameron, fully awake, jumped into bed with her.

She felt every shuffle they made. Their wheezy breathing slowed down, they couldn't find a comfortable spot next to her. When they sat on their back, they crossed their legs underneath the covers and kicked their foot, an anxious tic Avery never knew they had.

She didn't know a lot about them, now that they were sharing a bed. Their anxieties, their insecurities. She had a lot of them, too, some she needed to keep buried in Arkeh:na. If they resurfaced here...

She shifted the bed. *"Can I ask you a question?"*

They didn't answer.

Taking that as a defiant "I guess," Avery worded very carefully, *"When you were born...were you born a boy or a girl?"*

They stopped kicking their foot, her question freezing them in troubled waters.

"Because, well, in this world, Autreans look down on girls who kiss other girls. You know I don't care either

way how you identify, really, but if you were born, say, a boy, life would be a lot easier for us on the surface. We wouldn't have to hide what we have. We wouldn't have to fear what others say about us. We could be together."

A full minute passed. Neither of them spoke.

Had she asked too much? She'd never questioned them in this regard before. It didn't feel right, but if they answered in the way society wanted them to answer, maybe she could fix this broken part of herself.

Cameron sat up and dragged the blanket off of her head. Their eyes glistened with hateful tears. *"I don't know what your problem is with me right now, but if that's your way of making me appear more 'normal' to you or your parents, then work out this issue on your own, because I'm not helping you anymore."*

Her heart crumbled through her ribs. *"Cameron, I don't—"*

"Don't. I know exactly what you mean."

"No, I'm sorry. I really...I shouldn't have—"

"Choosing how I identify is so important to me, and you know that. I thought you were okay with it."

"I am. Really, I—"

"Whatever," they said, and slid off the bed to sit on the ground, away from her.

Avery covered her mouth in disgust. What'd she done? What'd she asked of them? She just needed to apologize and everything would've gone back to normal. What was wrong with her?

A single tear hit her pillow that night, a silent streak that cooled down her face into the midnight hours.

Chapter 20: Translation

They thought they'd read Avery right. Even though they were covered in dirt, even if they didn't have magical abilities like their Moeder, they thought she still liked them for them.

They'd been wrong.

Although, as they sat on her bedroom floor, tracing designs into the "carpet," they didn't believe that as much anymore. After she finally fell asleep, they realized something.

Something was *wrong* with Avery. She never acted like this in Arkeh:na, so shy and hidden into herself that they could no longer reach her. She'd acted like this during their first week of getting to know one another, but something had changed.

"You wouldn't understand, and I don't want to talk about it right now. It'll only make me sadder."

Cameron rolled that over in their mind. What'd happened to her? Had Bridget said something mean? Had she gotten into a fight? Had she hurt herself?

Dropping their head on her soft bed, they listened for that change in her breathing. They had so much left to say to her, but they didn't want to widen the crevasse forming between them. Did she really care about their gender enough to fight about it, or was there something more?

When the Moon passed through a cloud, Avery's room brightened up in bluish light. Cameron shivered and pulled their sweater over their nose. Maybe the weather was affecting her. If it was this cold in Arkeh:na, they'd never find a reason to be happy.

Oreo and Pumpkin whimpered downstairs and scratched at the wood for some type of attention.

Cameron, safe on the second floor, peered through the railing.

Pumpkin whined and pawed at the first step. They didn't know if Autrean dogs could walk up steps or if she wasn't allowed up here, but she seemed determined to see them again.

Cameron blinked twice at her.

She cocked her head and returned double the amount of blinks.

They checked that Avery was still asleep before tiptoe-ing down the steps. The dogs hopped in place when they saw them coming, and the orange one yipped expectantly. Avery had told them once that they'd never bitten anyone before, but they looked hungry for something.

Keeping on the second step for protection, they stuck out a hesitant hand, and the black and white dog licked their fingers before wetting their hand with kisses.

While a little pointy, they got why Autreans kept these as pets. If they bypassed the wolf-like features, they were pretty cute. Not as cute as bats, but still.

As they got reintroduced to their first dog, they met Avery's Fader's eyes from across the room.

They looked away. Keeping a Fader's gaze made them sweat. They didn't know how to act around them or new people. Avery had been their first.

The Fader said something to them.

Thinking they heard the word "food," they just said, *"No, thanks,"* and walked towards a window showing off the forest, the dogs sniffing behind them. The Fader had too many lights on on his side of the house, but next to the window, nothing but the Moon shone down on the land. They even saw a mountain. They wondered if it was Arkeh:na.

The Fader cornered them into the niche. He stood so tall and had enough authority to almost challenge a Grandmoeder's power. Cameron had just enough time to prepare themselves for their first Autrean conversation.

If he knew they couldn't understand English, it showed in his manner of speaking. He talked slower than when he talked to Avery. He used his hands, enunciated his words. How much he knew was expressed in his longer, more sophisticated words.

Between the nonsense, Cameron heard, *"I'm sorry"*— Avery said that a lot in English—*"but do you need anything? I can get you something to eat, or are you too cold? Do you need any pelts?"*

They were sure he hadn't said "pelts," but they felt more comfortable hearing that than "electric blanket." *"I don't need that. I don't sleep during the night, and I'm not hungry. I'm good."*

They were lying—they were not fine, and they were very hungry—but they didn't want to push their needs onto Avery's Fader, who looked more tired than Avery.

Smiling with tight lips, Avery's Fader said, "Okay," and almost ran back into the cooking area. Even though he worked as an excavator, it seemed like he enjoyed cooking above all else.

But what about Avery's Moeder? Currently, she was sitting at her "computer," surrounded by parchment and pens just like Avery described. She did something called "journaling," which sounded like record keeping, the closest parallel they had in Arkeh:na.

Her unfamiliar aura pulled Cameron into her space. They hadn't looked her in the eyes yet—a normal greeting when first introduced to a new Moeder—but they were curious, curious about how this world worked.

Curious about how two parents worked so close to one another without fighting.

They tiptoed across the shiny floor and looked around her shoulder. Oreo and Pumpkin backed them up from behind.

Avery's Moeder side-eyed them. Her computer was so bright that they had trouble believing she could actually see the words on screen. When they accidentally coughed on her, she turned and asked sternly, *"Do you need something?"*

Oreo and Pumpkin lowered their ears and slunk back to the living room. Unlike Avery's Fader, Avery's Moeder spoke quickly as if Cameron could understand her.

"I, uh, don't know. I don't speak English. It's hard to talk...without Avery."

The Moeder put one hand to her mouth in puzzlement.

It was true, now that they thought about it. They ventured to say more English words with Avery. They didn't feel embarrassed practicing around her. Now they felt like they'd just cursed out her mother.

She took out her phone and started typing. Her phone spoke in a strange voice. It sounded neither Arkeh:nen nor English.

She cycled through six or seven other languages, each asking a question in a mechanical voice. Each one sounded more foreign than the next. They were about to ask what she was getting at when one question pushed through the drabble.

"Do you understand this?"

It came from the phone, so Cameron didn't know who to answer: her or the machine. Guessing logically, they said to her, "Yeah. How did you do that? How does your phone know Arkeh:nen?"

Getting the result she must've wanted, she typed in another line of bright text. Her phone spoke: "It sounds like you speak Dutch, although some. I did not know you did not speak English. I did not know how much about you and Avery. Or your magical religion. I think it's good, as long as Avery is happy, however. She was worried about how I thought about you and her. Where do you live?"

A small bubble of pride swelled in Cameron's throat. "I live in a place called Arkeh:na. It's a Community underneath a mountain that's interconnected by *tunnles* and rivers. It's a beautiful place filled with beautiful *gemmes* and even more beautiful people. Avery used to come visit me all the time, but after getting stuck in a cave-in, she hasn't visited once. That's why I came here. I wanted to make sure she was okay."

The phone somehow translated what they'd said into English. Avery's Moeder read it over as if she'd be tested on it later. Her hand never left her mouth, keeping back her true words. She was definitely Avery's mom. She wrote: "I beckoned it. Thank you. Are you hungry or thirsty, or are you warm enough? Do you need something?"

Hearing the questions in broken Arkeh:nen was somehow more encouraging than having it questioned in broken English. "I can take some water, if that's okay, and something small to eat."

She read the translated line of text, then got up using her cane. Cameron went to help, but she lifted herself up without assistance. No wonder Avery was so strong.

"Ethan," she called out. *"Can you get the kid some water and some leftover mac and cheese?"*

"What happened? I'd just asked if she needed anything."

"I asked them. It's okay. And they're okay. More okay than I thought."

They took it as a compliment.

As they waited by the Moeder's computer for their cheesy noodles and water, their anxiety about the Autre world faded. They'd survived talking to not only Avery's Fader, but also her Moeder, alone, without help. Avery worried too much; they didn't hate them, they just didn't understand them.

The Fader put down their glass and bowl of noodles.

"Thank you."

"No problem."

If they could finally speak Avery's language, could they unveil this darkness enshrouding her? Could they get her to understand who they were and who she was both inside and outside of Arkeh:na? The possibility of finally talking to her about how they felt broadened as they repeated the words they heard her parents speak.

The Moeder came back with a cup of brown, steaming liquid and sat back down in front of her computer.

Cameron ate a bite of cheesy noodles. It still tasted bad, but they were getting used to the flavor. "Avery's Moeder?"

She held up a finger, pulled out her phone, and held it out across the table.

"Something's wrong with Avery. She's been getting upset with me, but when I ask what's wrong, she won't tell me. She says talking about it will only make things worse. Do you know what's making her so sad?"

She read over their translated words. "I do."

They smiled. "Then what is it?"

"I cannot say."

They lost it. "Why?"

She typed for a few minutes, backspacing her thoughts to clear up her meaning. "I do not want to tell you if she has not told you. It's a secret she does not think I know. It hurts her, until she asks for help. And, if you know my daughter, she does not do that easily."

Cameron felt like they were talking to their Moeder through her cards. "Can you at least tell me her secret, so I can better help her?"

"No, but I hope she tells you quickly. You are one of the few people who can help her."

They ate the rest of their cheesy noodles, then bowed to Avery's Moeder and Fader and climbed back up the steps. What did they have that could save Avery? If they knew, they would've given it to her by now.

They felt so drained that they crawled back into bed to rest. The way Avery breathed suggested that she'd woken up, but they didn't ask. Like her Moeder had said, she seldom asked for help. She'd rather entangle herself in her thoughts until she tripped over them and got hurt.

Tired yet not sleepy, Cameron closed their eyes to think. Their thoughts never left the girl pretending to sleep beside them.

Chapter 21: Apology

Avery awoke to the smell of maple syrup and the popping of bacon fat. Her mouth watered at a chance for breakfast in bed. When she turned to tell Cameron, she found herself alone.

She jumped out of bed half-awake and searched her room, the bathroom, and over the railing. Where were they? Had they left in the middle of the night? Yes, she'd said things she didn't mean last night, but that didn't mean she wanted them gone. She still needed to apologize.

She ran down the steps and almost tripped over Pumpkin. "Dad, where's Cameron?"

"Right over there," her father said, and pointed his spatula at the fireplace.

Cameron was sitting on the marble hearth, eating a plate of eggs and toast. Oreo sat on their feet for warmth. When they snuck him a piece of egg, Pumpkin whined and nuzzled her snout into their lap.

"She told me she lives in the woods," her father explained as he handed her her plate. "I asked if she wanted a ride home, but she said she wanted to wait for you to wake up."

Avery looked over to them to see how much of that checked out.

They still wouldn't look at her. Their head kept bobbing, sleep almost in reach. They must've stayed up all night.

Avery took their recluse seriously and ate at the kitchen island by herself. Memories of what she'd so boldly asked of them hit her like slow-motion bullets, each one piercing her slower than the next. She regretted everything. Their first sleepover should've been filled with movie watching and explaining what a movie was. Eating junk food, making terrible jokes, kissing...

And what had she done? Forced them to tell her what was in their pants when it never once mattered to her until now. Her self-hatred now equaled how much Cameron likely hated her.

Her father leaned over the counter. "Everything okay?"

She nodded without answering, which told him everything.

"If you want, I can drive her back home. I overheard what went down last night. I mean, I didn't understand any of it. When did you learn how to speak Dutch?"

"Dutch?"

"That's what your mother said. She said it sounds mostly like Dutch, with variants of other languages spliced in."

She split open her egg. "I never knew. It comes easily to me."

"Maybe you can take a class on it in high school. Cameron seems to understand you perfectly."

"Right now, I doubt that."

Cameron coughed over their meal. Oreo picked up his head and sniffed, then jumped back when Cameron started hacking out their lungs.

"I think they should leave now," Avery said.

"Okay. Let me get my boots on and clean the kitchen."

"No, it's okay. It'll be quicker if we walk."

"Shouldn't you leave a little later when it warms up?"

Avery calculated how much time she had left until the Sun rose. "No, she should leave now. Cameron."

Cameron stood up immediately, their body swaying.

She gave them one of her old jackets along with a pair of boots that barely fit. Cameron didn't complain. They hadn't even said good morning to her, and she didn't blame them. She hadn't said it, either.

"Are you sure?" her father asked as they left. "There's a storm coming down from Michigan. Should be here by tomorrow."

Avery let go a little smile. "I'm sure I'll be back by to-morrow."

"Well, with how much you spend in that forest..." He waved them out without saying more.

Avery led the way. All of her favorite trees and boulders had iced over. Gone was the chatter of birds and cicadas. A few squirrels slogged through the snow with them, but they scampered up the trees whenever Cameron coughed.

After they finished, Avery asked, *"Are you okay?"*

"How long does it take to get to Arkeh:na?"

"It's about ten minutes away."

Cameron panted into their turtleneck. *"I went that way,"* they said, pointing right, down to the farmlands. *"I didn't know where you lived. I must've circled the whole town searching for you."*

"I'm sorry."

"It's not your fault."

When the mouth of Arkeh:na came into view, Cameron walked past Avery and hid in its embrace. The Sun had started peeking through the pine trees. They must've felt content in natural darkness.

"You can keep the shoes and coat," Avery said, *"though you'll probably give it to your neighbors."*

Cameron cast a look into the cave, focusing on the rock separating them from their true home.

"Cameron." She forced herself not to look away. She just needed to say it. Two words, or more. Whatever they deserved. *"I'm sorry...about what I said last night, and for how I yelled at you in the caves. I know your identity is important to you, and I don't have a right to know anything you don't want to tell me. I'm sorry for how I acted. You didn't deserve it."*

Even though the Sun was moments away from hitting their cheeks, Cameron took a step out of the cave.

"I'm sorry," she repeated, trying to match the words in her heart. *"I'm sorry I hurt you."*

She'd memorized the path leading up to Arkeh:na, but Cameron hadn't. They stumbled on loose rocks as they jogged back to her, not looking at their feet, and threw themselves into her arms.

She dropped her head against theirs. This. This was all she needed: them, and the knowledge that even with her faults, they could still find a reason to come back to her.

"I was scared," they said into her chest. *"You weren't yourself. I thought something bad happened."*

"I'm sorry. Recently, I haven't been feeling like myself."

"Please tell me what's wrong. Tell me so I can help you."

She couldn't. Saying it out loud outside of Arkeh:na made it true, and she didn't believe she was strong enough to fight the fear it instilled in her. *"I don't feel like I'm a good person."*

"Why?"

Her bottom lip quivered. She'd pushed them away, and they didn't even think her a bad person for it. *"I don't know, but I'll get better, I promise. When I do, I'll come back to Arkeh:na, back to my normal self."*

"Please do. I want to be with you again." They stood up and kissed her cheek.

She closed her eyes and accepted them. *"Thank you."*

"Thank you for apologizing." Hacking into their hand, they patted her arm with reassurance that she'd come back and left for home.

Even though they couldn't see her, Avery waved until the rock fell back into place and they disappeared underground.

Just before leaving herself, she noticed a wet spot on her jacket.

A bloody, mucus-covered handprint stained the white of her coat, dripping down the seams like fragile icicles.

Chapter 22: Queer

With midterms behind her and a promising three-day weekend in sight, Avery had lightened her emotional load. She had the chance to finally go back to Arkeh:na, but when would be the right time? She'd apologized properly to Cameron, so she felt a little better, though this rotting feeling had yet to go away.

That Monday, she wasted the last few minutes of school wandering the halls. The buses had just pulled into the driveway and students were slowly gathering their belongings in their classrooms. Not too afraid of missing the last ten minutes of Spanish class, she sat on the foyer staircase and watched the clock tick by. Cameron was probably waking up right now, but after their sleepover, she wouldn't have blamed them for sleeping in. Even after she'd apologized, she still had trouble sleeping.

When the bell rang, she made herself small on her step. Students ran down the stairs or stood and mingled with their friends. The girls' and boys' basketball teams lined up at the front doors to leave for a game, wearing their shorts and loose tank tops. Avery caught herself staring and relocated herself appropriately.

She tried finding company with their school's fish tank. The small tank stood in the cafeteria hall next to the truant officer's room and the "cursed" bathrooms. "Cursed" because someone had allegedly fought a tenth grader in one of the stalls and punctured one of their lungs with a protractor. Avery didn't believe the rumor, but its unsavory past kept her and most students away.

But as she traced her fingers down the tank, the curse was broken. Someone left the girls' bathroom carrying far too many books in their hands, about to spill everything at Avery's feet.

Bridget collected herself, spotted Avery by the fish tank, then proceeded to walk towards the main hall as if to catch the bus. Then she second-guessed herself, admired her workload, and backtracked to Avery. "Are you catching a bus?"

Avery almost fainted. Was she planning these meetings from the future? She had to deal with her in both her classes and the cafeteria, so why was she here, now? She was so close to having her out of mind.

She fixed her bangs underneath her beanie. "My mom's picking me up."

"Oh, right." She restacked her books using the edge of the fish tank. A rainbow-colored fish watched her while others hid behind Avery, wondering why an eighth grader did so much for so little.

"I was, uh, thinking," she said casually. "Do you think you'd be interested in giving an interview for the school newspaper?"

"Oh, you got into the program?" she asked, knowing full well she'd not only gotten into the club but held more creative control than the teacher who ran it.

"Yeah. This month's theme is reinvention, like fresh starts to the new year. We wanted to get it out by early January, but..." She looked at the fish tank rather than the person standing in front of it. "We've been getting these small stories about wanting to do better at school and junk, but I think your story might, uh, make people want to read."

Maybe she really was a time traveler, or a spy who'd been following her into Arkeh:na without her knowing. She gulped. What had she seen? Had she seen her with Cameron? "What, uhm, what story?"

She turned away from her completely. "I didn't tell anybody. I know you're not supposed to do that. I know you're not 'out of the closet' or whatever."

She didn't know what she preferred more: Bridget knowing about Arkeh:na or her broadcasting Avery's private love life to the whole school. They were in a secluded part of school, but still, they were *out* in the open, speaking about "it" *outside* of Avery's brain. That one little word, it didn't matter what you did or what you wanted to be. It latched onto you and reshaped your whole identity without your permission.

She gripped the straps of her backpack.

"Henry James interviewed Jacob Sarkozy last week. We got a good story from him and his decision to join the theater club. He came out last year."

She searched for an adult, someone to save her.

"It'd make a great piece, having a girl's voice on the topic."

She fumbled out her tangled headphones and turned away.

"Avery?"

For so long she'd wished to get back on speaking terms with her friend, and now she wished for anything but.

When she returned home, she'd mute her on her computer, delete her number. Anything to get away from this conversation she'd never be ready for.

"Uh, hello?"

Her phone vibrated in her hand. Betwixt the yellow buses revved her mother's car.

Avery bolted for the nearest doors. She wouldn't talk about it. Not now. Not ever. Embarrassed, she felt like she was being peeled apart by hands she wished to caress. She wanted to feel whole for just a bit longer before she came undone like a knitted doll.

Bridget stopped her by pulling on her sweater sleeve. "I thought you were, you know, *queer*," she whispered, whispered like a dirty secret, something forbidden to be uttered within these halls. "Aren't you?"

Avery had been untangling her headphones, trying to silence Bridget, but she stopped. Her headphones ticked on the ground and spun in circles until they tangled together as one.

With a vacant expression, she picked them back up and rolled them around her iPod. She'd heard that word before. On forums, trying to find what word she clung to most. At first, she didn't understand its usage. Terrible people used it as an insult. But as she read through dozens of other people's discussions about why their hearts fluttered so, her eyes always lingered on that strange word.

The realization dawned over her. "That's me."

"Huh?"

"I'm queer. That's me." She laughed. "That's me, and that's okay!"

"Are you giving the interview now, because if you are, I can record you—"

Avery sprang through the double doors. Adrenaline hopped her into the car and flicked her feet together like celebrating cymbals. She got in so quickly that her beanie fell off somewhere between the seat and floor. She left it be.

"Hi?" her mother said in a question.

"Hi."

"Everything alright? You got in like a bear was chasing you."

She gave it a heartbeat of thought. She didn't have to tell her. Nobody had any business knowing. But her mother, someone she admired so passionately, she should've known. Even if it cost them their friendship. Even if Avery had to move in with her grandparents or get indoctrinated as an Arkeh:nen. It had to be done, because she wanted it done, and it had to be now, otherwise she'd never summon up the courage to again.

Her mother pulled out of the parking lot and onto the main road, taking Avery's silence as her answer.

Avery took a swig from her water bottle to wet her mouth. "Hey, Mom?"

She didn't take her eyes off the road. "Yeah?"

"I'm queer."

Her mother said nothing. She continued driving on. She itched her nose, then continued itching it like it wouldn't go away. Then she adjusted her grip on the steering wheel and checked herself through the rear-view mirror.

Avery's heart iced over in regret. Her heart sped up to an uncomfortable level, waiting, waiting. She hadn't planned on saying anything else. She just wanted a reaction, anything to end this terrifying silence.

Then her mother said, "Okay."

"Okay?" she repeated.

"Yes."

Avery's brain skipped on its tracks. "Huh?"

"Do you not want me to be okay with it?"

Well, no. She couldn't register it. She needed her mother to question her or hate her, react negatively, at least. Why else had she hidden this secret from her for almost two years?

"Do you think I'd hate my own child for something she couldn't control?" her mother asked. "I can be wary of her exploring caves and befriending magical people who don't speak English, but this? This's fine." She turned down a hill. "I was wondering when you'd tell me."

Was she a psychic just like Moeder Ellinor? "How long have you known?"

"Oh, for a while. I remember in third grade you told me you wanted to marry those two twins with the red, curly hair. One was a boy and one was a girl. When I told you that, you replied with, 'So?'. After that, I kept my eye on you and how you acted around your peers. It became obvious to me. Your father, not so much. Is it just girls you're into?"

"I don't think so."

"Okay." Stopping at a long red light, her mother reached over and rubbed Avery's leg. "I was worried for a while, ever since you stopped talking to Bridget. You lost your smile. I'm guessing she had something to do with this?"

"A bit."

"That's what I thought. Want me to tell your father for you?"

The gears in her brain finally started to turn. "Yeah. Yeah! Can I, uh, maybe go out into the forests when you do that, so you can talk in private?"

Her mother went to answer too soon, so Avery stammered out, "I-I've just been having a rough month trying to figure out a way to tell you guys, and midterms were really hard."

"You could've told us that."

"I know, but can I please go into the forest? *Please*? Just for an hour?"

"You know, you say that every time, but you stay out there for at least four, sometimes five hours."

"I'll be back before dark," she bargained.

"It gets dark at five. It's three."

"Mom, *please*," she begged. "I need to."

"Is it because of that boy, or girl...that *person* who slept over? What was their name, Cameron?"

Avery's face flushed.

"I guessed as much." She smiled. "Be home soon, okay?"

Avery nodded, though it was more to keep herself from sobbing over her mother's pristine car interior. Season after season she'd kept this part of her a secret. She'd taken a chance with Bridget and lost her because of it. She planned on moving out in case her parents ever opened her laptop and found what types of things she looked up. She expected them to denounce her as their daughter, but it was as easy as an "okay."

Most people like her didn't get an "okay."

She held herself back with her hand pressed tight over her lips, keeping back a smile ready to burst from her cheeks.

—✧—

Had it not been for the hidden black ice and fallen leaves, Avery would've run the whole way to Cameron's place. She had a time limit now, but she knew her mother was worrying the second after she ran out of the car.

Arkeh:na was as alive as she left it, with some differences. The collapse had decimated part of the artisan corner. Builders had created makeshift huts to keep their world running. From there, a few artisans waved to her. Some covered their mouths and whispered Cameron's name between their fingers. She paid those people no mind.

She parted through the *ville* with a bright smile not because she'd crawled back underground, but because she'd finally lifted the cover off of herself. Her steps became more lighthearted. She didn't fear where she'd step next. She even waved to some *shoppekeeps* before they waved to her. The woman with the monocle gave her a grim nod.

There seemed to be more people down Cameron's *tunnle* than usual. They kept whispering and running down the hall like they'd forgotten something crucial. Some slowed down to gawk at Avery, but continued on as if they hadn't seen her.

Avery's adrenaline and anxiety danced in her stomach as she slowed to Cameron's room. Neighbors craned their necks to see around Cameron's curtain, which was strangely closed. Others sat on the other side of the curved *tunnle*, rocking and covering their mouths.

"What's going on?" Avery asked them.

"Cameron—"

191

"They had an attack—"

"—and stopped breathing—"

"The psychics have them now."

Coughing broke through the curtains. A panic. Shuffling. *"Keep their head straight!"* someone shouted.

Avery pushed through the crowd and hooked a finger around the curtain.

Cameron was lying on the ground of their den, naked and sweating. Three Moeders sat around them with *gemme* necklaces snaked around their fingers. Someone had lit two branches on fire and infested the room with arboreal smoke.

Cameron's Moeder sat right beside them. She held one of the branches and was funneling its fumes into Cameron's nose. It didn't stop them from coughing up brown mucus.

Someone dragged Avery back. She fought her way back in, her body moving on its own, but then another hand much stronger than the first yanked her out.

She turned to Basil and Maywood with their hands still on her. Their eyes were bloodshot from crying.

"What happened?" Avery demanded.

"They're having trouble breathing," Maywood said.

"Then they need a doctor. They need to go to the hospital!"

"We aren't allowed in when the healers are working," Basil said, still hobbling on his hurt ankle. *"Come on. You can wait with us until it's over."*

Chapter 23: Stuffy

"Maywood, stop it!" Basil said. "You don't have to keep walking us home. I know the way by heart, even if I don't have my kaart like you."

"Then neither of us have to worry about getting lost, right, Cameron?"

Cameron stuck their tongue out at her as they walked through the ville. They'd just gotten out of school and were on their way home. Basil had been convinced that he didn't need his older sister to walk them home, but Cameron didn't mind. It'd given them the opportunity to tell Maywood all about their new identity.

"Call me 'they' from now on!"

Their "they," a new way to live out their life. It felt so right. Their teacher, Moeder Claire, had explained it to them so perfectly, too, like it had been made for them.

"Your new word's a little confusing," Basil said, catching up with them. "Are you sure you don't wanna be a girl anymore?"

"It's not like that," Cameron said. "It's confusing to explain, but I'm not a boy or a girl. I never was. I just want to go by 'they' now."

Basil gave them a skeptical look, then sighed and tossed his head back. "Fine, just don't get mad if I call you by the wrong word. It'll take some time for me to adjust."

"Me, too," Maywood said, "but I'm still proud of you."

"Thanks!"

When the time came, Basil and Maywood waved Cameron goodbye and went to their own den. Alone, Cameron smiled and jogged home, their school bag thumping against them like a dog's tail. Their Moeder might not have been home, but they knew their Fader would be. Sometimes after work he'd bring back fresh water or a new *gemme* he found in the Rivière. They couldn't wait to tell him.

When they got home, they found both of their parents waiting for them. They went to rush them with hugs and the good news, but an ominous air in the den dissuaded them.

Their parents weren't looking at each other. Their Moeder had a hand over her eyes. Their Fader had both hands over his face in some type of shame. What did their Fader have to be ashamed of? What was upsetting their Moeder?

For the first time in their life, Cameron was scared to talk to their parents.

Their Moeder clicked her tongue. "Well, go on. Tell her. Tell her what you told me."

"Tell me what?" Cameron asked, already unsure of responding to the pronoun.

Their Fader dropped his hands. "Cameron..."

Sensing that he didn't know where to start, Cameron eased him into conversation. "You know, this week in class we learned that you can call someone by 'they' if they don't feel like a boy or girl. I really related to that,

194

so instead of 'she', you can start calling me by 'they'. Isn't that great?"

The thought passed between their parents like choppy waters, hitting them hard enough to knock them over.

"Is that so?" their Moeder asked.

"That's...great," their Fader said. "I'm really happy to hear that."

Their Moeder shot him a dirty look. "Oh, don't act like you care about her—them—now."

Their Fader's jaw dropped. "O-of course I care. They're my own child."

"Like that matters to you anymore."

"What's going on?" Cameron asked. "Why're you two fighting again?"

Their Moeder sighed through the storm building in-side of her. "Your Fader's decided that he'd rather live away from us than provide for us. He's leaving for the surface tomorrow morning and never coming back."

Their Fader became rigid. "Why would you say it like that? It's not that I'd rather live away from you. I love you, Ellinor, and I love Cameron just as much. I just can't keep living like this knowing what's out there." He looked up past all the rock and soil that made up Arkeh:na. "I have to see it for myself. I can't live in the dark anymore."

Cameron tried to see what their Fader saw, but all they saw was their den's roof, the den that'd protected them for generations.

They reached out for him. They couldn't say goodbye. They'd just discovered such a big part of themselves. They should've shared this experience with him for years to come.

Their Fader, already packed, left their den without a goodbye. Cameron wailed for him to come back, but their throat burned with hot air.

Their Moeder wrapped her arms around their naked body. "You're okay," she whispered. "Just keep breathing."

"But I'm not okay," they wanted to shout. "We're not okay," but their Moeder kept squeezing until she materialized through their breaking body.

They came to slowly, not fully aware they were asleep at all. They had a horrible headache and shaky eyesight. Then they smelled a high concentration of cedar and flowers that watered their eyes, making it even harder to see. Had they gone to see Avery and collapsed in the forest? Had they traveled into the afterlife, death finally taking them? Their throat and chest hurt enough to assume so, but after taking a few breaths, they proved themselves wrong.

When they finally had the strength to open their eyes, they awoke in their bed. They were sweating underneath three furry blankets. Someone had lit candles around their bed as if they needed light to sleep. It did provide a sweet smell to their den, but they didn't want to seem indulgent to their neighbors.

They sat up, their head filled with sand, and coughed. It alone drained away the rest of their energy.

Avery, who was sitting in the corner of the room, awoke with a start, snorting back the spit in her mouth. She sat beside their Moeder, who was cross-legged and flicking through her tarot deck. It looked like she was giving herself a reading. She shuffled the cards together after seeing Cameron up.

Avery scrambled towards them on her hands and knees. "Are you okay?"

"Yeah. When did you get here? What time is it?"

"About eight-thirty Avery's time," their Moeder said.

At the mention of the time, Avery yawned.

"Why're you here so late? Won't your Moeder get upset?"

"I went back home and told her I was sleeping over your house. She wanted to argue, but I told her you'd gotten into an accident and that I wanted to be here when you woke up."

They rifled through their memories. All they remembered was their Fader turning their back on them. They hadn't even seen his face. It was a blur, just like the past several hours. "What happened?"

"Noel said she heard you wheezing, then came in to find you clutching your chest," their Moeder explained.

Noel was one of their neighbors who lived with her three kids. "I don't even remember seeing her," Cameron said.

"She said you were coughing up blood and not responding. She didn't know what to do, so she ran to get us. Me, Yuna, and Willow cleansed your body with smoke and fire."

"Which you shouldn't have done," Avery interrupted.

Their Moeder continued as if she hadn't heard her. "You ended up passing out after we calmed you down. Avery and I have been waiting for you to wake up."

Avery straightened her shoulders and met their Moeder's eyes. Had she ever done that before? Had she done that with anyone before? "I know you said you didn't want to hear this—"

"And I still don't." Their Moeder reached for Cameron's cheek. They gave it to her, shocked at her level of intimacy.

"I think you have to hear this. You aren't supposed to inhale that type of smoke if you're trying to clear out your lungs. We have something on the surface called an inhaler that can help open up their lungs—"

"They don't need that. What we provide for them is enough."

Exasperated, Avery said, "But it's not. They're getting sicker. You said so yourself."

Cameron pulled back from their Moeder to see Avery properly. They'd never heard this side of her before, so standoffish. No, so impassioned. They never thought someone could get annoyed by their Moeder, but Avery sounded beyond annoyed.

She stood up and over their Moeder. Sensing the challenge, their Moeder did the same. They almost stood as equals, both in height and in the fierceness in their eyes. "I was just like you. I looked past Cameron's coughing for a long time. I didn't think it was right to stick my nose into a culture I wasn't brought up in. But their sickness is a direct result of them—of *all* of you—living in Arkeh:na. Arkeh:na is killing you, and you need to leave before it takes Cameron away."

Their Moeder placed a hand on her hip. "I thought this sudden noncompliant attitude of yours was a result of my child's sickness. I was willing to leave such insolence un-noticed. I'm shocked at your willingness to keep this up."

Cameron knew Avery wasn't familiar with those larger Arkeh:nen words, but she didn't waver. Maybe she'd taught herself the words to stay on-level with their Moeder. "I'm not trying to be rude. I'm giving you the truth and the facts that living here is not healthy and that it will hurt you more than help you."

Their Moeder began turning away, but Avery stepped in front of her. "Please. I know Arkeh:na means a lot to you."

"Then stop—"

"But I *have* to speak my mind now. I love what Cameron and I have together. I love them."

Cameron inhaled. She'd never said those words before.

"You need to take this into consideration. If you want Cameron to live past thirty, even twenty, you need to think about finding a different place to live. You don't even have to leave the mountains. You can live in the forest." She licked her lips, knowing the lie when she heard it. Cameron knew they couldn't live in the forest without an Autrean messing with them. "Please. Think it over. Think about Cameron."

Their Moeder withdrew the anger in her eyes, falling back into her composed self. "We're done talking about this."

"No—"

"I said we're done," she said, and shoved the curtain aside. "Maywood and Basil asked me to get them once you awoke. I'll be right back."

Cameron heard her stomping feet all the way down the *tunnle*, her anger still at the surface, unable to be buried. "What happened between you two?"

Avery threw up her hands. "I'm trying to convince myself that I can talk to a brick wall. I'll get through to her, though. I have to." As she spoke, she wiggled down into Cameron's bed.

Cameron scooted back. A fire had been lit underneath her bum. "You seem strong about this."

"I am." She pushed back the hair from her eyes. She'd lost her beanie. "Your sickness isn't contagious."

"I don't think so."

"Good," she said, and kissed them.

Fate must've really hated them. It had to be now, of course, that Avery felt the most comfortable with kisses, when they felt the sickest. Fate just worked out like that, always slapping you with cruelties only to sprinkle the wound with momentary gaiety.

They fell back, bringing her forwards. She had so much vigor now, nothing like the other times they'd kissed. She wanted this more than anything. She was hungry.

When she pulled back, she smiled. She even licked her lips.

"You...you said you didn't like this," Cameron panted, trying to catch their breath.

"I'm okay with it now," she confessed. "I'm not afraid anymore."

Cameron breathed a few more times to get themselves back up to speed, then kissed her with newfound strength.

As they kissed her, a thought passed through them. Maybe, if they had Avery and everyone who filled up Arkeh:na's *tunnles*, maybe they *could* relocate to a new home to "get better." They felt silly thinking this; it was an impossible idea no one would ever entertain.

But with every kiss they shared, the possibility grew and grew until it never left their head.

Chapter 24: Out of Your Comfort Zone

Cameron's kisses could only quiet Avery for so long.

"You can't live your whole life in these caves. Look at what it's doing to your body."

"But I'm fine. This's normal."

"You puked three times last night! Do you know how many times I've puked this year? Not once. The last time was when I was seven after I got off a rollercoaster."

"I don't know what that means."

Thus went the next two weeks, and the more she visited Arkeh:na, the more she realized how sick these people lived. Their knees, bow legged. Their eyes, yellowed. She'd been so impressed by this world that she hadn't noticed how deteriorated their bodies were. And Cameron didn't think it a big deal.

They did get better, though. They stopped fainting whenever they sat up from bed, but they were bedridden during the times they could keep themselves awake.

After passive-aggressively fighting with them one day, Avery left to walk off her fumes. Ever since living through their escalating sickness, she'd typed up a thousand-word document on her phone listing out every sickness she spotted. Face pores, unexplained rashes, bloated joints. Question marks surrounded each new bullet point.

—◇—

Back at home, Avery kicked her feet above her. How could she, some thirteen-year-old girl with anxiety, move three hundred people out of a home their ancestors had built up for more than three hundred years?

"They're doing a disservice to their ancestors if they died in a crumbling hole," she murmured into Pumpkin's fur. She was on her bed, problem-solving this dilemma. She grabbed her pen to write that down, but her thoughts turned to jelly before it touched paper.

Stuffing her mouth with sour gummy worms, she scribbled out the sentence she'd been working on and grumbled more at Pumpkin. "What if we build them cave-like houses? They can be close to the forest, too, just ventilated and clean."

Pumpkin licked her face.

"How about we get a community center to house them until we figure out a way to get...the state of New York to house three hundred homeless..." She stopped herself. Throughout her research, she discovered that New York had 100,000 homeless people. She didn't think 300 cave people would catch their eyes unless it was for shock value and TV interviews.

"Avery, dinner," her mother called from downstairs. "Bring down the dogs and feed them."

Avery hid her laptop underneath her pillow. Even after she came out to them, she still hadn't told her parents the truth about Cameron. If she told them now, they might ban her from spelunking and hand everything over to the police, people who couldn't speak the language as well as she could. She couldn't let that happen, but she couldn't let Cameron's health worsen.

Both her mother and father were home that night. Her father just kicked off his work boots and was booting up his computer to continue working. Her mother, like always, had her favorite seat at the end of the kitchen table, her laptop open, her phone charging by her mouse.

"Make your plates," her mother said. "Food's in the oven. I'm hitting a deadline for a paper. Turns out my editor decided to go to Martha's Vineyard for the weekend and not answer her emails. Now I'm scrambling to reach her for this edit on abandoned warehouses in Manhattan."

Abandoned warehouses. That could be a housing option for the Arkeh:nen people. They just needed to set up plumbing, electricity, a company to clean out the mold and cockroaches...

Avery sat beside her mother, careful so as not to spill her spaghetti over her work. She had piles of it strewed over the table. So many articles for reference, so many multicolored sticky notes labeling her drafts.

Avery's fork clattered to her plate.

"You alright?" her father asked.

She shoveled down two bites of spaghetti. "Yeah. Hey, Mom? I was, uh, hiking in the woods, walking north like normal, when I discovered this cave—"

"Oh, no," her mother said. "No more caves, Avery, please. Your father was just telling me about more cave-ins happening at work."

"One got us unexpectedly. It almost buried a guy."

"I-it was before I fell. I was exploring it for a few minutes, then I started getting a really weird feeling, like I was being followed. So I turned on my flashlight and explored the darker tunnels. When I hit a dead end, I heard something. It was like..." She paused, drawing in her father and raising her mother's eyebrow. "...*people* were talking to me through the walls."

"That's strange," her mother said.

"Maybe you heard a hiker's voice reverberating off the walls."

"I don't think it was a hiker. They were speaking a different language."

"Why didn't you tell us this before?" her mother questioned.

"Because both of you were gone when I came back," she lied. "You were so busy with your work and I was so, uh, tired and flabbergasted that I just went to bed. Wouldn't that be a great story to tell your firm? Maybe I can bring you in and you can check it out yourself."

Her mother held up her pointer finger. "First: I don't take on writing pieces without discussing it with my editor." She put up a second finger. "Second: I can't hike up those long trails like you can, and third—" A third finger. "I'm not going into some creepy cave that's pitch black to follow voices who whisper to passerbys. I'm not letting God take me that easily."

"If you want, I can take you on easier trails," her father suggested. "I can make sure they're safer."

Slightly discouraged that the reporter had no interest in this story, Avery ate her dinner in silence. Even if she brought them on board, she still needed to convince the Arkeh:nen that they needed to leave. She didn't know which one scared her more, and which would be more impossible to achieve.

—◇—

The next day, she walked down into Arkeh:na with her head buried in her phone. Knowing Cameron wouldn't be up at two in the afternoon, she turned right, walked over the *Rivière's* bridge, and made sure not to disrupt the psychics' dens with her heavy steps.

Maywood was carefully threading silk through her spinning wheel when she walked in. *"Hi,"* she said. *"I don't think Cameron's up yet."*

"I guessed as much."

Basil walked in from another room on a single crutch, trying to carry a box with one hand. He barely made it before Avery swooped in and helped him.

"Thanks," he said.

"No problem. How's your leg feeling?"

"It still hurts."

"Still hurts, huh?" She looked over Maywood's legs. *"Maywood, have you always had leg pain?"*

"As long as I can remember, yes. My Fader was unusually tall, and I unfortunately carried on that gene."

Avery consulted her notes.

"What're you doing with that phone?" Basil asked. *"You're going to blind yourself."*

"I'm trying to convince Cameron that these pains you're suffering from are a result of Arkeh:na. I want you all to become Autrean."

Maywood, startled, dropped her cane on the floor. *"What do you mean?"*

Avery picked it up. *"Living in a cave your whole life isn't healthy. It's like being trapped inside your room all day with no Sun. You'll get sick."*

"We're fine the way we are," Basil argued. *"Aren't we?"*

"No. If you lived on the surface, your ankle would heal faster, Maywood could get braces for her legs, and Cameron could take medicine for their cough."

Basil touched the bandages around his ankle. He flinched, hissing back the pain.

"I love Arkeh:na and do want to see it grow, but I don't want one cave-in or sudden sickness to ruin what you've all created. I know it sounds scary, leaving a place you feel safe in, but society can benefit a lot from what Arkeh:na has to offer. You just have to be brave enough to take the first step."

She hadn't meant to go as far as she did, but once she finished, Maywood and Basil lowered their heads in thought. The two other workers in the room cleared their throats, letting Avery know they overheard her.

As she went to clarify a few of her points, a knock came from outside.

Cameron stepped in. They were wearing one of Avery's turtlenecks with their bear pelt wrapped around their shoulders. Their nose was red and scratchy like they'd been itching it all day, and their bedhead looked messier than normal. It shaded their sleepy eyes.

"Are you feeling better?" Maywood asked hopefully.

"Worse," they said. *"The Grandmoeders called me down. I don't know what I did, being that I've been in bed all month."*

"Let me come with you," Avery said.

"You can't."

She got up anyway and waved to Basil and Maywood still thinking over her offer. *"I can walk with you. You can barely stand."*

Cameron leaned on the doorway. *"I can walk by myself."*

"You're such a bad liar," she said, and hooked her arm around theirs.

The chilly air from the Grandmoeders' Den welcomed them. All five Grandmoeders sat accounted for, all sitting on their blanketed beds decorated with candles and *gemmes*. Grandmoeder Geneva smiled at them when they entered.

Grandmoeder Nai curled her upper lip. *"We didn't call you."*

"Cameron's sick. It's hard for them to move around right now."

"They don't need your help," she said, but her words meant little to Avery. Her need to help them stay alive a few more years made her ignore the sweat dripping down her armpits.

"I had a feeling they'd come together," Grandmoeder Geneva said. *"I've heard they don't often leave each other's sides."*

"They didn't talk for nearly a month," Nai reminded her.

"Yes, but I'm sure they didn't leave each other's minds, did they?"

Avery didn't know if she expected an answer. Her beating heart should've made it obvious, but she wanted to believe the Grandmoeders couldn't hear her heartbeat from across the den.

"Anywho," Grandmoeder Geneva said. *"I wanted to ask you two a few questions I'm sure you have the answers to. Avery, your head seems quite full these days. Do you wish to let go some of those thoughts?"*

"May I?" she asked, glancing at the other Grandmoeders.

Grandmoeder Geneva held out her hands. *"You may."*

She looked at her phone for fifteen or so seconds, quickly scrolling through her notes, then tried regurgitating them in a sophisticated manner. She hadn't expected this presentation to come so soon. Luckily, she had Cameron to help define the untranslatable words like airborne illnesses and neurological disorders. Saying it in English would've been easier, but it felt unjust in anything other than Arkeh:nen.

She listed off all the problems cave dwelling could give them. She mentioned that most Autreans would be kind to them, but that they would need an adjustment period to understand them. The idea of hospitals, the benefits of fresh water. Everything that could help them understand their situation, she explained with facts and love. While she spoke, she wanted to hold Cameron's hand, but they'd only distract her. She kept her argument focused on the ones whose decisions affected the whole.

When she had no more arguments to bring up, Grandmoeder Geneva, like always, smiled. *"That's quite a case you've created on your own, and to speak it in our native tongue, too."*

"She has the vocabulary of a child," Grandmoeder Nai commented on, though her aggressive stance had disappeared.

"I see your concerns, my child, and I do agree with a lot of your points. I, too, have had unease about our living conditions since I was small."

Cameron gasped at that. They clutched their pelt close to their heart, hanging on to her every word.

"To see my children perishing in, as you put it, avoidable ways scares me for our future. Even if some of us might not be able to admit it, we know that our sicknesses are becoming deadlier than we can handle and need to be addressed."

She lifted her hand from underneath her blankets. Her bloated, age-spotted joints shook from arthritis. "We all face the troubles Arkeh:na has beset us with. While it's been our home for generations, it seems time we think carefully about what we cherish more: our ancestry, or our future."

"Let me pose a question," Grandmoeder Nai said. "Why do you want to help us? Is it just because of Cameron?"

"Cameron was the first person to introduce me to Arkeh:na. They showed me how loving and magical it can be. Now I want to be able to protect it just as much as I want to protect them."

She closed her phone. "Your traditions, your families, all of that can stay with you. It's just your place of living that needs to change in order to keep those traditions alive. Living here used to keep you safe, but now it's killing you, and you owe it to your ancestors to keep their efforts alive."

Grandmoeder Geneva nodded along with most of the other Grandmoeders. Grandmoeder Nai lowered her head and kept her arguments to herself.

"We shall discuss it together," Geneva said. *"You two are free to leave now."*

To Avery's surprise, Cameron took her hand first and darted for the exit. She needed to be careful not to step on their dragging pelt.

When they shut the wooden door, she exhaled. *"That went okay, right? Did I mess anything up?"*

Cameron crumpled against the wall just above the *gemme*-lit lantern. Their blanket snagged on it and gave them a cover to cry under.

Avery knelt beside them. *"What's wrong?"*

Their sniffling escaped their curled fists. *"I...I don't want to leave. It's our home, it's everything we know. If we leave now..."*

Having no other way to console them, Avery rubbed their back in nothing but understanding and support.

"Why do we have to leave?" they asked.

"Because you'll die otherwise."

"I'd rather die here."

"You can't. I still have to marry you."

"I don't know what that means," they said, and hugged her back, readying themselves for an unpredictable future.

Chapter 25: Arkeh:na's Decision

Cameron knew Avery had reshaped the Grandmoeders' hearts when Grandmoeder Nai gained a twinkle in her eye. It took a lot to persuade her into doing anything she didn't want to do, but Cameron saw it, and so did Grandmoeder Geneva. Geneva was the final call, the decision maker, and Avery had sold her on the idea of uprooting their whole world just to heal a common cough.

That morning—Avery's evening—she left with a short kiss to Cameron's temple, encouraging them that everything would be alright.

Everything she told them sounded right as rain. They *did* need to leave, and the quicker they did, the better. For them, for the Grandmoeders, for every single child born from here on after.

But Cameron would've rather died here than risk coming out to the world.

Leaks about the Grandmoeders' decision swept through Arkeh:na like one of Avery's "viruses." Misinformation spread about what might happen. They *might* be forced into igloos, they *might* live on the streets. The biggest rumor, one Cameron almost believed, said they'd all

live with Avery until they built a new mountain for themselves by hand.

Avery promised that her Moeder and Fader would help,
but how? 314 Arkeh:nen needed to pack up and leave to
someplace unknown. They had trouble believing two Autreans could help with something they weren't involved
with.

Cameron sat awake in bed, thinking all of this over.
They knew they shouldn't have been angry with Avery.
She had their best intentions in mind. She wanted them
safe, and they wanted her happy.

After the Grandmoeders gave their final verdict, Cameron cried into their bear pelt for days.

Nobody really talked about the move. Everybody just
started packing up like mindless drones obeying their
queen. One morning, Cameron awoke to their neighbors
stacking their belongings outside of their curtain. They
later found out this was trash, memories that could be
thrown away. Cameron saved what they could.

Soon enough their Moeder stopped working. Dozens of
Arkeh:nen craved her advice during this turbulent time,
so much so that she exerted herself. Drained of power, she
came back one day and stayed for the rest of the week.

She and Cameron slept together for the first time in
years, her back pressed against theirs, her gentle snoring
bringing Cameron back to infancy. After their Fader left,
her snores had been the only way they could get to sleep.
Now, knowing she couldn't work partly because of them
kept them awake.

One night, as they tried not to shift the blankets, their
Moeder touched their shoulder. "Rest."

"Sorry."

"Everything will be alright. Ever since I met Avery, I knew this was going to happen."

"But where're we going to go? '*Hospitals*'? '*Rescue centers*'? The Autreans don't even speak our language. They won't understand."

"That's a very valid criticism that I hope Avery's put more thought into than she's led on."

Cameron bunched up their pelt close to their face. "Moeder, I'm...I'm scared. I don't want to leave."

"I know. Emotions are the hardest to deal with at night. That's why we always want someone close to us before we go to bed." She continued massaging Cameron's shoulder.

"Moeder, do you want to leave?"

"Absolutely not."

The way she said it so bluntly made them smile a bit, a half-smirk they could barely raise from their pillow. "Do you hate Avery?"

"I hate that she's right, and I'm fearful of how much you've grown attached to her. Feelings are something I've mastered through my readings, yet they've become a burden to me. They're something I'd rather avoid than confront. You've helped me overcome a lot of those fears, especially after your Fader left."

"I've helped *you*?" They couldn't believe it. "How?"

"Ever since I met him, we had a falling out that could never be fixed. We were on a bridge that continuously swayed. That swaying only grew once we had you. His desire to leave contrasted my need to stay underground. When he left, the bridge snapped and I was left stranded with you. After that, I closed myself off. It was you who rebuilt my bridge and connected me back to love. When I heard Avery arguing about leaving, I was back on that

214

bridge, but instead of having you in my arms, you were on the other side with her."

Now their lightheadedness didn't come from just their sickness. It was like being back in her psychic room as a child, hearing her cry and realizing that she was a complex human with even more complex emotions. "I had a dream about him right before you and Avery argued."

"Isn't that the way," she said. "All dreams connect us to the now, waking up when we ourselves need to be woken up." Her restless hand found its way into Cameron's hair. "Get some rest. Avery promised to meet with us tomorrow to discuss how this'll go. You'll find peace with her."

"I'll try," they said with a cough, and stayed up for most of the night.

—✧—

The bustle outside their den woke them up. Arkeh:na had woken up about an hour earlier than usual, too nervous to sleep, too nervous to finalize packing.

They found their Moeder sifting through their *gemme* collection. Most of what could've been brought to the surface was already packed outside. Only the bulkier parts of their *gemme* collection remained.

Their heart skipped. She'd never touched them before. "I-I'm going to sort through them now," they said.

"You've collected quite a lot here," she said. "Some of these are quite rare."

"They are?"

215

She handed them one of their least favorite *gemmes*. "This one is quite drawn to you. It holds a lot of positive, healing energy. Have you had it for a while?"

"Yeah, but every time I tried connecting to it, I never felt anything."

"You feel calmer when you're around them, don't you?"

"Yeah. I like collecting them."

"Then how are they not doing their job?"

Cameron rolled the ruby *gemme* between their fingers, then pocketed it for later.

"Some of these *gemmes* might feel better if they were left here," she then added. "They're able to live here. We cannot."

"I know."

"But they'll still love you, even if you're apart from them."

They bit their lower lip. "I know."

She wrapped one arm around them. "It'll be alright."

Their eyes welled up. Before they could let go against her, the bell within their den, as well as every bell in their *tunnle*, rang.

"The Grandmoeders said they wanted us to be at the *Centrum*," their Moeder said.

Still not quite ready to leave, they double-checked the remainder of their *gemmes*, making sure they had every last important one. There had to be something more they could do.

They raised their head to Nuvu still hanging on her grate. They cooed for her. "Nuvu, let's go."

She clicked her tongue at them.

"We have to go," they said. "Come on."

She stared her owner down.

Cameron reached higher. She never listened. "Nuvu."

"Cameron," their Moeder whispered. "I think Nuvu has to stay. Bats belong in caves. Arkeh:nen...Humans do not."

Cameron grit their teeth as they reached higher and higher, waiting for her to fly to their hand like they'd trained her to do, but she didn't. Chirping softly, she wrapped her wings around herself and got comfortable on her perch.

Cameron dropped their arms. The stubborn blood drained back to their fingertips.

"Don't hold it against her," their Moeder said. "She belongs here."

"We do, too."

She touched the middle of their back, helping them leave. After giving Nuvu a tearful look, they finally, finally, turned away.

They and their Moeder stood in the curtainless doorway. Their den looked so empty now. The places where Cameron's *gemme* boxes had sat open for so many years left imprints in the Earth. Even without blankets, their bed was probably still warm enough to crawl back into.

"Once we move, we can visit here all you want," their Moeder said. "I'll take you back on trips."

Cameron touched the edges of the walls, then erupted into coughing.

"Let's go," she said, picking up their belongings. They'd wrapped them in bundles and boxed them in crates. "Fresh air can only help you at this point."

"So you say," Cameron said, but followed her down the ladders and bridges regardless.

About 200 Arkeh:nen stood ready at the *Centrum* with their belongings. Toddlers ran around their parents, who gossiped about the move with their neighbors. The other 100 or so were still packing away their homes. They lined the walls, whispering their reservations.

The *ville* and artisan huts had been swept clean. All the wood from the shacks had been repurposed as moving boxes. Even the fires meant for cooking food had been doused. What was once a thriving village now looked like a crowded prison cell.

Their Moeder guided them through the sea of whispers to Basil, Maywood, and their Moeder. Their Moeder had found something to argue about with Basil. Basil looked to be holding himself back. "I'm fine."

"You're not. Knock it off and let me carry your things."

When Cameron's Moeder came into view, Basil's and Maywood's Moeder lowered her voice and yanked the box out of Basil's hand.

"Hello, Exia," Cameron's Moeder said. "I'm sorry I haven't been around to give you your readings. I know this week must've been stressful for you."

She closed herself off with her shawl. "It's been terrible, knowing I have to do all this moving by myself. Maywood and Basil here, trying to work in the conditions they're in? Where're the Grandmoeders, and the Autrean girl?"

Nearby Arkeh:nen turned around to listen for any news they could get.

"She'll be here soon," Cameron said. "She usually comes around this time."

"Do you need to sit down?" Maywood asked them. She was sitting on one of their moving boxes, resting her tired legs.

Cameron didn't answer. They'd been listening to the talk around them, then the loud cacophony of sound in general. Like piercing through a misty film, the sound grew louder and louder until someone screamed.

Cameron didn't know where to move first. It sounded like water was rushing in on them from all sides, but they knew it was rock. Tumbling, free-falling rocks aiming to bury them. These cave-ins, these sinful strings of fate breaking off at the seams, you couldn't prepare for them. Everything happened in seconds and destroyed life even quicker.

The Main Exit *Tunnle* went first. A cloud of rock, a screech, and then it was gone. Then the ceiling collapsed. It caved in and splashed into the *Rivière*, burying the artisan district. Bats flew into the air. Babies cried. Arkeh:nen screamed for the Grandmoeders' safety as they ran from being crushed.

Maybe this was Arkeh:na's final way at saying goodbye. Knowing its inhabitants were deserting it, it felt only just to bury them all in one shared grave.

Cameron ate their words. Avery had been right. They'd wanted to die in Arkeh:na, but they never wanted Arkeh:na to *kill* them.

They went for their Moeder's hand, but she was gone, swept away by the running crowd. Lost, they fell on their back and watched helplessly as Arkeh:na collapsed on top of them.

Chapter 26: The Operation

Avery was screwed. What was she thinking? The weight of 300 lives rested on her shoulders, and now she had a pop quiz tomorrow in math.

She'd lied right to Cameron's face. How could she help them? Sure, she'd laid out a plan. She'd laid out six plans, each one better than the next, but was that enough? What would she do with the sick, with people like Maywood who needed extra care? All of them needed medical attention to some degree. Who would pay for that? She'd read online that the state would care for some homeless people if their conditions were serious enough, but the Arkeh:nen weren't even citizens. They could be refused care because of that.

But she had to do it. Everyone was probably waiting for her at the *Centrum* by now. It was her fail-safe in case she got cold feet and pushed the migration back another week. Hundreds of people were now waiting for her to act, and she was waiting for her mother to pick her up.

She'd skipped last period to hide in the bathroom. What was she doing? She just wanted to sink through the floor and pretend that Cameron would be alright without her help.

The bell rang and jumpstarted her heart. In one hour, she'd be responsible for three hundred lives.

She picked up her bag and walked out of the stall. She stared at herself in the mirror, swayed a bit, then lost her stomach in the sink. It burned coming out and smelled of sour food, but she withstood the feeling until she had nothing left inside of her. Spitting out the warm sludge around her gums, she looked back up at herself and saw the same girl, just a little sicker.

She washed down the grossness, made sure none of it had stained her shirt, and left. She'd hidden in the first-floor bathrooms near the lobby so nobody would walk in on her, but as she was halfway out the door, she knocked shoulders with someone in more of a hurry than her.

Bridget gasped and caught the pile of books about to spill out of her hands. Avery caught one and their fingers touched, but instead of getting flustered, her nerves stayed at critical high. Maybe she'd hit her limit and little nuances like touching her old crush's hands didn't faze her as much.

"Hi," Bridget said. "I was searching all over for you. I was wondering when you wanted to do that interview. My teacher said he wanted it done this week."

"I'm actually going to be really busy for a while." Avery scanned the parking lot for her mother's car.

Bridget stepped in front of her. "If you want, we can do it during a study hall."

"Yeah, that sounds fine." She fished out her phone and read over her notes. She'd typed out a speech for her mother to get her on board with Arkeh:na, but she'd edited it so much that it would've been better for her to ad lib it.

Bridget fidgeted with the corners of her books. "Actually, I was wondering if you wanted to hang out this Saturday to do it. I have to go grocery shopping with my father, but maybe we can...schedule something at my house." She looked away as she said it, then looked at Avery to see if she'd heard her.

Avery paused, thinking over such an enticing offer. She'd deleted her number. Her username was blocked. She'd prepared on avoiding her until graduation and then throughout all of high school. Could they really start over like this, staying friends?

She opened her phone back to her notes. "I don't think I'll have a lot of free time for the next three or four...weeks."

Bridget drooped. "Oh. Well, maybe we can hang out when you're not busy. Can I have your schedule for next month? My family was planning a camping trip during Valentine's Day—"

Avery went to text her mother when the buses churned out of the parking lot. Parked underneath the flagpole was her mother's car.

"I-I gotta go," she said, fixing her bag on her shoulder. "Sorry. I'll text you."

She didn't turn back. Racing between the buses, she jumped over the curb and flew into her mother's car.

"Hey," her mother said. "What exciting news do you have for me now?"

"Would you believe me if I said it was something bigger than me coming out?"

Her mother's face turned serious. She went to turn off the car. "You've been crying. What's wrong?"

"Nothing. Can you drive? I need to tell you something important, but I don't want...Can you please start driving?"

Looking at her skeptically, her mother pulled out to the main road. "Did you fail something? Did you get detention?"

"It has nothing to do with school."

"Did you get in a fight with someone?"

She braced herself for a thousand questions she'd have to answer a thousand times. "Cameron—"

"Are you pregnant?"

Her jaw dropped, but the sheer illogical threads that tied her to Cameron made her smile for the first time that day. "We can't get pregnant."

"Oh, okay. I don't..." Slightly embarrassed, she let go of the tension in her shoulders. "It's always good to ask. What is it, then?"

She had to tell her soon enough, and she'd told her about her sexuality and nothing had gone wrong. What else did she have to lose? Her mother was one of her closest, smartest friends, and any other questions she had could've been answered by her.

Feeling slightly better, Avery took a deep breath. "Cameron lives in a cave in the middle of the forest. It's the reason why I've been going out hiking so often. They live there with about three hundred other people. It's a society. They call it Arkeh:na."

Before her mother could react, Avery continued, her heart thumping. "And they're sick. They're getting sicker. It's because they've been living inside of these caves all their life. I convinced their elders to leave, which's very hard for them because they've been hiding for so long. Now they need to leave and I need help getting them out."

Her mother kept driving. She drove down Main Street, took a turn where the farmlands met the post office. Her breathing picked up as she opened and closed her mouth like a gasping fish.

At least Avery hadn't hidden this from her for years. She couldn't have withstood holding in two secrets for that long.

"I knew it."

Avery gulped back a mouthful of spit. "What?"

"When they slept over that one time, I got to talking to them."

"What—How?"

"I brought up an online translator. It was patchy, but it worked. They speak a type of Dutch, and they told me something about a cave and their people. I thought it was a translation error. I didn't know what Arkeh:na was. I tried researching it, but nothing came up."

"So you've known for this long?"

"W-well, it depends. Are you serious?"

"I'm not lying, so, uhm...yes, I'm serious."

Her mother gawked at the road, blinking rapidly. "So you're serious? They really live in a cave? There's, what, three hundred of them, you said? That's not possible."

"Well, it's a system of caves, like how ants connect their tunnels from underground."

"How long have they been living like this?"

She guesstimated. "Probably since the 1600s, maybe a little more. They don't know what cars do, if that helps you paint a picture of how they live."

The truth left her mother gaping for words. "Well...so, what do we do now? Do we call the police and have them take care of it?"

"T-they didn't do anything wrong," Avery defended. "They don't know how our society works. They're not citizens."

"It's not only that. There's a whole bunch of procedures and rules that need to be followed. We'll have to get in contact with...I don't even know. Where are they in the forest?"

"Up the hill."

"I can't walk that far. We'll wait until your father comes home before we start calling people. The police should be involved. If three hundred people leave the forest, unable to speak English, they'll be questioned by the police regardless, or at least the state troopers. You said they're sick?"

"A lot of them are, yes."

"Then ambulances should be dispatched. But first, I want your father to confirm this for me, make sure you aren't losing it in those caves. God, I knew my feelings about those mountains were true. Mother Instincts are never wrong."

"But I can't wait that long. I promised Cameron I'd be there after school. They're all packed and ready to leave."

"Well, they'll just have to wait. You shouldn't have waited this long to tell me this. We'll have to take this slow. Are you sure this can't wait until tomorrow?"

"I'm not sure. I'll go out and ask."

"Good. In the meantime, I'll call your father. He'll never believe me. How is this going to work?"

With the weight of Arkeh:na's secret finally off of her mind, Avery sighed. The hardest part was over. Now all she had to do was pry Cameron out of those tunnels.

Chapter 27: A Change of Heart

Their world trembled beneath them, a fearful animal too scared to move. Even when it stopped, Cameron's dirty hands continued to shake. They were a part of this destruction. They shouldered its pain.

They didn't move straight away. One because they didn't want to risk hitting their head. They couldn't see very well and couldn't tell how close they were to a pointed rock. Two because it kept them grounded. Whatever was left of Arkeh:na, as long as they could touch the Earth, they had a place to stay.

But they couldn't keel over and get buried by their own home.

Confused outcries sprouted from the ruins of Arkeh:na. Dust poisoned the air and made it hard to breathe. The unnatural smell of wet soil replaced the odor of the Arkeh:nen *tunnles*. As the rumbling subsided, not many babies or children cried. It made their mothers cry in their wake.

Someone touched them. The feeling of their calloused hand was enough for Cameron to bury their face in their bosoms.

"Moeder." They reached out for her through the dust. She was on the ground.

"I hurt my hip." She struggled to stand and failed, breathing so abnormally that Cameron considered if they were truly talking to their Moeder at all.

"Don't," they said. "Lean on me. I'll carry you."

"*You* carry me?" she said, almost chuckling before coughing. "Where is everyone?"

"I-I'm here," Maywood said off to their left.

"Where's Basil?"

Cameron didn't know who said it first, because both they, their Moeder, and Maywood asked it at the same time. They didn't wait long to hear an answer.

Basil grunted as he shoved something away from him. "I'm here."

Maywood pushed aside their fallen world and helped him stand with her cane. Their Moeder came out next, who seemed in better health aside from her shawl, which was now stuck between the rocks. She hugged both of her children.

They'd survived, but those whose fates were not accounted for, the ones who guided them...

"Where're the Grandmoeders?"

The single question sent everyone into a frenzy. Here, there, people darted around the rocks to locate their beloved leaders. Some even climbed over the new mountains in order to see farther out. While all of them took the hands of those calling out for help, their real loyalties lied with the women buried somewhere beneath their feet.

Cameron braced themselves and lifted their Moeder up. She kept off her right leg entirely.

Maywood knelt beside her. Her own Moeder's hand wouldn't leave her shoulder. "Where're you hurt?"

"My side, and my back. I'm alive. Look for others."

"How is this real?" Basil asked, his hand digging through his hair.

Cameron's Moeder held her own head. Either she had a headache or something else was upsetting her. Did she know this would happen? Was she experiencing a swell of new possibilities that would affect so many? Was she scared? Was she in pain?

Cameron nuzzled their head on her good shoulder. In return, she ran a hand through their hair, then sat on a rock to catch her breath. She covered her mouth with her shirt.

"Moeder, may I go search for others?"

Their Moeder stared at them from around her knuckles, never breaking eye contact with them. And neither did Cameron. If they didn't cough, if they could fake being healthy for a few seconds, they could go out and save others.

She nodded once, and Cameron pulled their shirt over their face and set off. Their Moeder shouted advice and warnings at them, all of which they knew and practiced regularly, but they took it to heart. They didn't run. They didn't panic. Avery had once told them that sometimes, if her laptop was covered by her covers, it would overheat and shut down until it cooled off, so Cameron imagined themselves as a machine. They took their time. They breathed out of their mouth. They were seconds away from shutting down, but they still had a few more tasks to complete.

Families cried as they tried organizing those around them. Most clung to one another and kept asking the same questions to everyone's vague answers. Cameron wanted to go to each of them and give them false senses of security, but they couldn't dwell on those wants.

On they went, zigzagging around boulders. They discovered more families that'd been ripped apart and those who'd just been reunited. While they shared a collective comfort, their eyes kept searching through the unturned rock.

Cameron stopped. A tingle ran down their spine. They tried to shake it off, but the feeling yanked on them like a child.

It brought them between the Grandmoeders' *tunnle* and a collapsed part of the ceiling. While the *tunnle* looked relatively safe to enter, the feeling instead led them to the crushed pile of rock.

From the rubble, a weak, elderly hand tried digging itself free. "*Help.*"

Cameron ran and tripped right before the hand. They rounded its bulging veins and wrinkles. It felt deathly cold, but it shivered with determination to survive.

A tear fell from their eye. "*Help!*" they screamed, then coughed, cleared their throat, and raised their voice. "It's Grandmoeder Nai! She's hurt! *Help!*"

A dozen heads sprung up and rushed to their aid. Muscular men and women bounded over and started digging without question. One lifted up a heavy plank to give others room to dig.

Grandmoeder Nai had lost her blankets and had a purplish bruise on her temple. She couldn't stand without the help of three large men, but once she found her feet, she didn't fall.

"Are you hurt?"

"Do you need anything?"

"Can you stand?"

"Wait," she wheezed, and pointed behind her.

Cameron's eyes narrowed into the small opening of rocky dirt. They went on their hands and knees to go in themselves, but the larger-bodied Arkeh:nen jumped in one by one. They shuffled around the debris and made a sizeable hole to carry out Grandmoeder Geneva.

Grandmoeder Nai's blanket was wrapped around her. Her leg was twisted. Her head sagged as if asleep. When her rescuers asked her questions, she didn't respond.

Cameron didn't know when one tear morphed into sobbing, but when they fell beside her, they cried into her side.

Her hand touched the top of their head. She barely felt there at all, a snowflake melting into their hair.

"I'm sorry, I'm sorry," Cameron apologized. For what, they didn't know.

"Do...not apologize," she whispered. "You did...everything right."

They wanted to believe it, but they couldn't stop imagining a world without their grandmother. Fate couldn't take her away now, not when it'd already taken away their home.

"Is there any water?" one person asked. "Does anyone have any food or bandages?"

"The falls collapsed," another said.

"Here, take my shirt."

"I have a few pieces of jerky."

"They can't eat that. Someone chew it for them."

"I'll do it."

In a half hour of panicked searching, they tried digging out every Grandmoeder they could. Some were worse than others, some more conscious than others. The worst injuries came from Grandmoeder Geneva, who kept falling asleep whenever someone stopped talking to her.

But even with her injuries, she wouldn't let Cameron be her crutch. Neither would their Moeder. It was like they cared more for Cameron's well-being than their own, which was something they couldn't wrap their head around. The only way they understood it was relating it to how Avery treated them. They wondered if that came from being "stronger" than the other person or from love.

They'd been sectioned off from two-thirds of Arkeh:na. The ones with the loudest voices relayed information to those deeper in the *tunnles*. Cameron's side had three Grandmoeders, many of the psychics, and the remains of the Falls and Main Exit *Tunnle*.

"Where should we go?" one person—Barron—asked, which created a wave of questions with no clear answers.

Cameron's Moeder sat on the ground during these discussions. Whenever someone asked about her hip, she clenched her jaw and lied, saying she was fine.

Cameron didn't have the strength to call her out on her hypocrisy. Maybe it was genetic, this stubborn worry they had for everyone other than themselves. What they couldn't keep to themselves, however, was the easiest answer most Arkeh:nen had yet to discover.

When the questions died out to mere mumbling, Cameron announced, "I can find a way out."

Half of them turned. A third of them eyed them with justifiable doubt.

"The *tunnle* where Grandmoeder Nai and Grandmoeder Geneva were found is still stable. If we want to leave, we should leave through there."

"But some of us are too hurt to move," one person argued. "Your own Moeder can't even walk."

Cameron remembered to inhale calmly so they didn't cough. "Staying here is too dangerous. The ceiling could collapse again, and I know these *tunnles* better than"— They stopped short before they insulted anyone listening—"my own den. I can go by myself or with others, but I don't think we should leave anyone behind."

Just then, a sizable rock broke off from the ceiling and rolled towards Grandmoeder Nai. Basil jerked and pulled her out of the way just in time.

Grandmoeder Nai whimpered and held onto her grandson for safety. He blushed with conflicting emotions.

"It's not safe either way," Cameron pushed, "but please, if someone can just follow me and see, I'm sure it'll be safe."

"How do you know?" one person asked.

"I don't. It just feels right to leave now."

When no one stood up or grabbed their bags to journey with them, Cameron lowered their head. They shouldn't have said anything. They needed to come up with a clearer and safer plan, as a group.

Their Moeder stood up. "Let's go, then."

The crowd reacted in the way Cameron wished they'd done in the first place.

"Are you sure?"

"Ellinor, your hip."

"My child is right," she said, "and if no one wants to believe them, fine. I, however, am going."

"I go...where my children go," Grandmoeder Geneva whispered, and startled those taking care of her.

A murmur passed through the crowd. It sounded like they didn't want to go, but they'd rather disagree with Cameron than with their Moeder or Grandmoeder.

"Fine," one of the older men said. "I'll go. We'll search the *tunnles* and see if there's a path to the surface."

Cameron went to follow him, but they all waited for Cameron, they who hadn't once looked at their *kaart* to find a new way home. They trusted them. They relied on them.

They'd never felt such a feeling before.

Cameron bowed in appreciation and let them gather what few possessions they still had before moving out.

As they led them to the *tunnle*, Basil limped over and patted their back. "I was waiting for you to say that," he whispered. "You know these *tunnles* better than our own ancestors. If anyone can do this, it's you."

They waited for him to sprinkle in more compliments about how he favored them, but he left it at that, smiling at a truth he truly believed in.

Keeping that close to their heart, Cameron leaned down and crept into the *tunnle*.

They fell to their knees. They hadn't expected it, as their coughing hadn't been an issue for much of the collapse. Their legs just gave out. Their vision blotted in colors and stayed blurry even when they blinked them several times. When they came to, Maywood was crouched by their side, a blur of brown and white.

"Are you alright?" she asked.

"...Yeah," they lied, and continued on. After all, they could've found their way through these *tunnles* blindfolded.

Chapter 28: The Rescue Mission

"I never knew these mountains were so icy. Avery, I don't know how I feel about you walking up here in the winter."

Avery rolled her eyes at her father and called for her dogs to keep up. She convinced her parents to bring them along on this family trip to Arkeh:na. She even persuaded her mother to come. To her, she needed to see it first before she made any decisions. To her father, Arkeh:na was still a myth orchestrated by his imaginative daughter. With how much they grunted to keep up, Avery's somewhat positive mood began melting with the snow.

But still, while doubt lingered in the air, they'd agreed to come along. They hadn't left the house together as a family in months, so it was good to hear them behind her for once instead of listening to her own footsteps fade away into the trees.

"How deep underground does this place go?" her father asked, making small talk.

"I'm not sure of the dimensions, but my ears pop whenever I go down the Main Exit *Tunnle*."

"And you said they hardly see the outside world?"

"Only those who're allowed to leave can. They're mostly scavengers, borrowers who take supplies from our world to use in theirs."

"And how is this world held up?"

"I'm not sure," she said. "Rocks? Why?"

"I'm just concerned. A world like this where so few people see the light of day, I'm surprised they're still alive."

Avery slowed to a stop, Oreo stopping faithfully behind her, Pumpkin running up ahead. She knew something was wrong the minute she didn't see the top of the mountain. She double-checked to see if she'd fallen off course, but she knew these hills. She'd passed the fallen log, crossed over the vernal pond. She was here. Arkeh:na was not.

The mountain no longer kissed the sky or even the tree line. It was slumped now, halved like when Mount St. Helen had erupted sideways. Rocks littered the ground. Dust coated the air.

Arkeh:na had caved in.

"My god," her mother whispered.

Boulders tumbled from the mountain's slanted side and crushed newly budding oak trees. Her father gripped her arm tightly, but *she* wouldn't have been crushed.

She found herself sitting on a boulder, piecing reality back together. Oreo had his head in her lap while her father spoke to her. "Avery? Avery, hello? What's wrong?"

Wrong. This was wrong. Where was Arkeh:na? She needed to do something—scream, call for help—but she couldn't will herself to move.

Staring out into space, she locked onto the shape that used to be the Main Exit *Tunnle* buried underneath rubble.

She pushed herself up. One step, then another. She dug out the entrance she'd rested in so many times. With each handful of dirt, rocks came down and buried her work.

She pressed her ear against the rock. When she heard nothing but the birds outside, she hung her head. Pumpkin, having no other way to console her, licked her face.

"Avery, what's wrong? Talk to us."

"I don't..." She couldn't speak. Unable to answer, she instead ran around the mountain and checked the hole she'd escaped from after the first cave-in.

It'd collapsed into itself.

She held her head. Paramedics, the police, news crew. It would take days, maybe even weeks to dig out all 300 Arkeh:nen, if there were still 300 Arkeh:nen left to save. Had she brought her phone, her walkie? Would she have a signal out here?

Her fingers moved on their own. She was always afraid of calling 911 on accident or on purpose, but she didn't realize she was talking to an operator until they repeated a question to her. She also didn't realize she was sprinting down the hill with Oreo and Pumpkin until she slipped on an icy puddle and skinned her elbow.

"Hello, 911, what's your emergency?"

Her tears got in the way, but she forced herself to calm down and retold the last few months to them as quickly and as truthfully as possible. Finding Arkeh:na, meeting Cameron, keeping all of it a secret. She confessed that she didn't want people to think she was strange because of her underground secret.

She got that feeling from the operator, who kept repeating what she told them in questions, but she couldn't let this fear overtake her. For Cameron's sake, she needed to be strong, or act like it. She wondered if there was a difference.

—◇—

Having two police cars ride up to her house intimidated her, but having a blaring fire truck and two ambulances come up the hill afterwards left her quaking. It felt like she'd done something wrong. She didn't know what to say to the officers, only that Cameron, her friend, had been trapped in a cave-in, along with many others.

They brought up three side-by-side ATVs that fit four people each. Apparently the officers took her claims seriously. She didn't know why that surprised her. At this point, she didn't think anything could catch her so off guard.

It felt odd, guiding a group of adults up the mountain in a machine that sounded ready to fall apart every time it turned. Nobody knew where Arkeh:na was, and her directions of "turn left at the birch tree" and "see that boulder? Follow it until you see the other boulder," undermined her confidence. Her father filled in the gaps where he could, but with his limited understanding and Avery's stuttering voice, the officers began sighing at this fairytale.

As they reached the crumbled mountainside, the officers took off their hats to understand just what'd happened in their woods.

"You said your friend's in there?" the firefighter asked. "In the mountain?"

"I checked the perimeter and couldn't find a way in," her mother said. She was on line with another 911 operator.

"And how many people are in this family again?"

"300," Avery said. She knew it sounded ridiculous to them, but she didn't care and started hunting for a new entrance.

"Excuse me," said the firefighter. "You said 300? Are 300 people—?"

She dug around the exit hole hiding the fallen oak tree. At this angle, the dirt she thought was undiggable caved in. It spilled out into the niche where the dead tree lay, revealing a spacious point of entry.

Forgetting about the police and firefighters, Avery slipped through the opening and ran down the fallen oak.

"Hey, wait!" one of the paramedics warned. "It could all come down on you."

Apart from where it'd collapsed months ago, most of the tunnel remained intact. She didn't have to force her shoulder through many tight crevasses. Many of the off-shoots had been demolished, though, masking the air with dirt and dust.

"Avery, wait," her father said, but she couldn't. She thought the mountain couldn't have been excavated, but she'd found a way in. If she could find her way back to the *Centrum*, she was sure to find surviving Arkeh:nen there. Or maybe the Grandmoeders' Den. If it was still intact, it'd likely be a safe haven for them.

"Avery!" Her mother struggled to fall into the cave. When a firefighter insisted that she stay behind, she said, "If you think I'm leaving my daughter in there, you're denser than the rocks around us."

Avery came up to a dead end. She searched for some type of landmark, but the cave-in had destroyed all the ropes and ladders needed to get through the tunnels. She needed to go back around and keep searching. She was losing time.

An officer went to ask another question when they stopped quite suddenly. They, like Avery, stopped breathing to listen to the echoes of the cave. As everyone quieted down, they lifted up a single finger, asking for silence.

Through the wall, a faint scratching was trying to dig itself free.

Avery got to it first. She banged her hands on the wall, then started digging, all the while screaming Cameron's name. Dirt caked underneath her fingernails. Her hands froze from the wet earth. If she could save one Arkeh:nen, just one...

Hearing more and more voices begin to bloom, the firefighters took out their axes and began chopping away some of the rocks. An officer radioed for a helicopter. Avery's mother gave up her cane as a makeshift shovel.

"*Cameron!*"

A noise burst through the rocks, and before anything else sealed them away, a very pale, very small and dirty hand struck out.

Avery didn't need any confirmation on whose hand it was. She knew this hand, had held this hand, and had imagined putting a *gemme* ring on this hand.

Cameron, their Moeder, Basil, Maywood, and about thirty other Arkeh:nen stood baffled in the tunnel. They'd all been hurt in some way, bruised and bleeding from their escape. Cameron's Moeder held Grandmoeder Geneva on the ground. Basil's and Maywood's Moeder had

240

Grandmoeder Nai standing. It looked like she didn't want assistance, but as help arrived, she broke out into a thankful smile.

Cameron fell to their knees, exasperated. They touched Avery as if to make sure she was really there.

To clear up any assumptions, Avery knelt beside them and hugged them, laughing herself to tears.

Chapter 29: Hospital Visit

Cameron had never seen such alien Autreans before. They came at them like demons, wearing heavy armor and glossy masks. One tried to touch Grandmoeder Nai, but Basil stepped in front of her to protect her. Not understanding Arkeh:nen customs, they backed off and let Avery take charge.

She stayed with Cameron the entire way, translating English to Arkeh:nen and then Arkeh:nen back to English. The Autrean "officers" wanted children and elderly out first. When they wanted Cameron to leave, Cameron walked backwards deeper into the *tunnle*.

"It's okay," Avery told them. "You don't have to be scared."

They knew that. Truly, they did. They'd leave any minute now, they'd show her.

As night came, more Autreans gathered into the forest. Machines Basil noted as "helicopters" circled the trees and thudded the air with energy. Large "cars" and "news trucks" drove up the trails. They promised medicine and care for all. With the children crying and the adults coughing, the Community had no choice but to leave for this "better life."

Those less adamant about leaving were given blankets to wear and warm food to eat. First the Grandmoeders were taken away, then Basil and Maywood. Cameron watched on as each family member left them.

"Let's go," Avery said, holding out her hand. "You'll be okay."

Her Moeder and Fader stood behind her, the Sun setting on them like curious angels. Others had their heads poking around the hole. Everyone was waiting.

They took a step out, then another. Then one of the frailest strings on their heart pulled them back.

Their Moeder was standing back in the shadows. Arkeh:nen dirt muddied her face and hid her almost like a ghost haunting an abandoned home.

Avery's Moeder stepped around her daughter and held out her hand. She looked as scared as Cameron felt, her fingers trembling slightly. Their Moeder, was she scared? She hadn't spoken once since the Autreans came.

Their Moeder's eyes caught on the Sun. They shined a moment, just a moment, before she interlaced her fingers with Avery's Moeder's. Then, together, as a family, they exchanged the shadows of Arkeh:na for light.

And noise. Dozens of Autreans crowded the hole, which had been stickered with yellow ribbon and Autrean writing. They called out Cameron's name and held out strange devices to them and Avery. They were persistent, talking over one another and getting louder and louder. What was their job in the Autre world? What were they doing with their time?

Cameron shielded their Moeder from them and helped her onto the rocks.

Before them, the forest dipped into a ravine they'd never noticed before. Harsh reds and yellows colored the sky and clouds like in Avery's pictures, but better, richer.

They smelled pine trees and wet grass. A deep purple tinted the mountainside. The snow, which had just begun to melt, twinkled at Cameron's feet like magic.

They felt a cough trying to force its way out, but they couldn't do it. Taking in the sunset, they stayed as quiet as possible and prayed that they saw this sight as often as Avery did.

But they'd wished for too much. The blotting blackness overtook their vision and stayed. The noise of the news reporters faded. Their legs numbed. Sense after sense failed them until they lost the will to stand. Tipping sideways, they landed face-first into snow, a bed too soft not to sleep in.

It felt like someone had drugged them. Their body was heavy and their eyes were watering uncontrollably.

Two tall Autreans stood above them wearing face masks. The ground kept shaking and equipment kept rattling, but neither of them seemed to mind. They asked Cameron questions as they fiddled with something on their floppy arm.

Too tired to answer, they fell back asleep.

The second time they opened their eyes, they felt cold and shivery even though a heavy blanket was keeping them warm. The high feeling returned and mixed up their thoughts. Brighter lights and a man's voice, and Cameron fell back asleep with their hands numbing to a concerning level.

—✧—

The final time and Cameron was more awake and aware of their surroundings. The room came into focus and they could feel the stable ground beneath them.

They were on some sort of elevated Autrean bed in a lax position. The bed had a railing on both sides and weird bumps beneath the blankets. When they uncovered themselves, they found thin tubes connected inside of them. One was blowing cold air into their nose. The other was buried in their arm. It stung when they tried to take it out.

Panic set in. The air in this room smelled too clean. What'd happened to them? Why were there tubes inside of them? What kept beeping?

When they tried to peel off the transparent tape on their arm, a woman came in wearing blue clothes. She smiled at them like they weren't under distress, then walked to a chair Cameron hadn't noticed was there.

Avery was asleep in it, her long legs spread out in front of her and head tossed to one side. When the woman touched her, she yawned, stretched, and spoke to her. Cameron heard the words "sick," "breath," "weak," and "Cameron."

"Avery, take these things off me," they begged. "It's hurting me."

After speaking with Avery, the woman in blue took out a bottle filled with pebbles and offered it to Cameron.

"You need to take these," Avery explained. Her voice dragged on every syllable, sleep stirring her words. "It's medicine. It'll make you feel better."

Unconvinced yet unable to disagree with her, they took the pebbles and ate them.

Avery chuckled. "You were supposed to swallow them whole."

The woman said something to both of them, smiled, then exited through a large white door.

"Avery, what's happening to me?" they asked. "What is this?"

"You're in a hospital a few hours outside of Foxfield. It's filled with healers."

"That woman didn't look like a healer." They held their head with their tubeless arm. "My head hurts."

"I know. You've been here for a few days. I've been running back and forth between rooms trying to decipher everything between Arkeh:nen and English."

"Where's my Moeder, and Basil and Maywood? Where're the Grandmoeders?"

"Almost every Arkeh:nen was sent to a hospital, and this hospital could only hold so many. They didn't split up families, though. Your Moeder's down the hall, and your Grandmoeder's a floor beneath us. Basil and Maywood are in Utica."

Cameron closed their eyes in pain. They didn't get it. Arkeh:na was so much safer and better than this. There, they didn't have to worry about separation or hospitals or eating things as opposed to swallowing them whole. They didn't hurt this badly, only mildly so.

Avery swiveled her chair closer to Cameron's bed. Against the fluorescent light, they saw the color underneath her eyes. Her blinks lasted seconds, each one longer than the last.

"Are you okay?" they asked.

"I'm just glad you're here. We've been able to help so many people from the Community, from giving them hearing aids to braces for their legs." As she spoke, her head bobbed. "We also found out the name of your condition. I was right. It's asthma. You'll need to use an inhaler from now on. And you need glasses. Your eyesight is...really crappy." She closed her eyes. Cameron didn't know if she needed a moment to reorganize her thoughts or if she'd truly fallen asleep, but they didn't want to disturb her. Even they could sense how little energy she had left.

While she slept, Cameron looked out the windows overlooking "New York." They saw what looked to be Arkeh:na's mountain, now a mere blur of blue and green behind thousands of tall buildings. Trees, streams, roads, cars, they saw everything thriving against the skyline.

They didn't have to squint to take it in.

Chapter 30: St. Agatha's

Avery never thought people would remember her name. They never could at school, and if they did, they called her Aida or Amber, never recalling her true name. It'd taken her a few years to come to terms with her lacking charm, and by senior year of high school, if things hadn't changed, she told herself not to take it personally.

Seeing her face on national TV the next day destroyed that horrible self-image of hers.

In that short week, everyone in America knew about Avery Marlow, the thirteen-year-old middle schooler from Upstate New York who'd discovered one of the world's largest underground communities. They knew about her school, her interests in hiking, and her relationship with the Arkeh:nen Cameron Quinn, all of which made for "interesting topics" during interviews.

People from all around the world wanted her interview. News trucks drove cross country to speak with her, only her. Not her parents, not her grandparents. Her mother tried to coach her on answering interview questions in a professional manner, but with Cameron still in the hospital and all the Arkeh:nen separated in different hospitals across New England, Avery had no attention span. She'd tried to look up ways of dealing with interview anxiety, but she concluded that nobody got over it and it was terrifying every time.

She did, however, memorize the types of questions she'd receive. About a dozen times she'd told the camera the estimate size of Arkeh:na, her friendship with Cameron that'd developed into something more, and the surprising taste of dandelions and wild mushrooms. Amongst all the questions, the dandelion answer attracted the most attention.

One month after the extraction and the interviews calmed down. They almost ceased to exist, and Avery slowly felt herself falling back into routine. She had final exams coming up, Bridget's birthday was next week, and Cameron was now just a few blocks away.

One day after class, Avery sat on her laptop with the webcam on, video chatting with a news station down in Manhattan. The familiar logo she always saw on TV made her nervous, but she'd talked with this host twice already. It untethered her from her nerves.

"I've been told they're all doing well," Avery said. "There're still a few in critical condition and some are still waiting to get surgeries, but many of the children have been reunited with their families in group homes and homeless shelters."

"And where are all of these '*Arkeh:nen*' in relation to New York?" the news reporter asked.

Avery smirked; she hadn't heard *that* pronunciation before. A linguist had translated a funky spelling of the word, but to Avery, she just repeated the Arkeh:nen way of saying 'Arkeh:nen.' "About seventy percent of them are still close to Foxfield. Some have been stationed in downtown New York, but officials have been working hard on coupling everyone back together into their Community."

"Well, we hope everything turns out well for the future," the news reporter said. "One more question for you, Avery: What've you been up to now? How're you planning the new year now that you're about to enter high school?"

"Well, after this interview's over, I'm going to pack up a lunch and bike to Cameron's place. We have a date together."

The reporter laughed. "Well, let's not hold you up. Thank you for speaking with us today."

After saying goodbye and doing some wrap up with the host, Avery turned off her video chat and sighed. She'd hidden her shaky hands better than last week's interview.

"That was really good," her father said from behind the TV. He had a pot on the stove for dinner. Her mother, who stood right in front of her at the kitchen counter, was juggling emails on both her laptop and her phone.

"New York Morning News just sent another email asking you for an interview," she said, "and they want you to write a blurb about...something. I don't know. I can't keep track of all these emails."

"I thought you said you liked all of this publicity," Avery said, gathering her lunch from out of the fridge. For today's date, she'd packed two sandwiches, one apple, and two cracker packages. After some back and forth with Cameron, she found that this was the healthiest and most favorite snack for them.

"Not all of *this*!" her mother said. "I'm losing it with all these—I got another one! Another one, from some news agency in Connecticut. I'm going to lose my mind. I did *not* sign up for this when I decided to have a child."

"I'm leaving, then," Avery said. "Love you."

"Bye. Love you. Be safe."

"Bye, my lovely, chaotic fledgling."

Forty-five Arkeh:nen had been placed in a nearby medical and rehabilitation center in downtown Foxfield. After scrounging up spare cots and money donations, the facility opened their arms to a portion of Arkeh:na without much hassle. Many people didn't believe that these cave people should've been given so much free care. A lot of protests in the streets wanted Avery's family to pay for everything. But with a lot of extra protests, funding, and general human empathy, the Arkeh:nen people got the care they deserved, including Cameron and their friends.

Avery rode up to St. Agatha's Home of Healing and parked in her usual spot. Aside from hospital care and living provisions, St. Agatha's offered educational programs, too. Teachers and volunteers came in every other weekday to teach classes about the Autre world. Soon, it became a give and take; while the Arkeh:nen learned about Autrean life, the Autreans learned bits about Arkeh:na that hadn't been disclosed on the news. How the Community understood *gemmes* and how many languages it took to form Arkeh:nen became subjects of interest for international scholars. Suddenly more and more people wanted to speak Arkeh:nen *with* the Arkeh:nen people, wanting to learn as much as they could.

St. Agatha's also helped the Community learn through a more idealized lens. Its backyard had gardens and walkways and a fence to keep out news reporters. The Sun rose and set over the mountains and gave the Arkeh:nen needed doses of vitamins. It took time for some of them to leave, but with the help of encouraging nurses, the Arkeh:nen walked out sheepishly in their donated coats and scarves. Cameron liked sitting underneath the tree near the pond, listening to the sounds of their new world.

When Avery entered the building, the receptionist, Mrs. Way, greeted her. "Hi, Avery. How was school today?"

"Good, thank you. Is Cameron doing okay?"

"I heard they were upset about a failed English quiz, but they've been talking a lot about you," she added with a smile. "They say that since you go to school so close, you should come visit more often."

"I visit four times a week!" she said, and walked through the revolving doors with her ID card.

Down the hall, she passed by Maywood and one of her aides. She had math homework in her hands and was playfully arguing out one of her answers. After a few x-rays, her doctors had placed her in a wheelchair until her limbs gained back their needed strength. With how hard she was gripping her pencil, she was either growing stronger, or her homework was overtaxing her.

"Hi," Avery said in English. "How are you?"

"I am...good, thank you," Maywood said. "How was...*How do you say 'school'?*" she asked in Arkeh:nen, and Avery gave her a hint.

"School?" she asked in English. "School? It's weird. A weird word. 'Weird' is weird. Our word is gooder."

"Better," her teacher corrected, and tapped Maywood's paper.

"I try," she said.

"It's okay. Try again."

"How're your legs and arms?" Avery asked.

"Good...Better," she said. "Physical therapy is hard, but it works."

"That's good. I'm glad."

"You want Cameron," she said, noting the jump in Avery's knees. "They're in the trees, the park."

"Thanks," she said, and ran through the patio doors to find them.

She stopped halfway through the doorway, finding someone much more surprising waiting for her.

Outside in the patio garden was Bridget, her father, Basil, and his mother, all talking around a bed of flowers.

Bridget looked up when the glass door closed. "Oh. Hi."

"Hi?" Avery said in a question. "I didn't know you two knew each other. At all. What's going on?"

Basil looked to his mother before blushing and standing up. "I told my doctors about my father and, after taking some of my blood, they found him." He gestured to Bridget's father. "Meet my dad, and my new sister."

Moeder Exia played with her bangs to hide her own blushing face. Bridget's father took to fidgeting with one of the flowers nearest his cheek.

Taking in Bridget's father, a tall Spanish man with a thick beard, and Bridget, who always look like a super-model in her eyes, she did see the resemblance, but she couldn't have imagined how close an Autrean could look like an Arkeh:nen and vice versa.

"Yeah," Basil said, reading her face. "She said you and her are friends from school. Is this the girl you mentioned before?"

"Y-yeah, she is, and we are," she said, still stunned.

"Families here are strange. I'm not used to how this world operates, but it's been fun getting to know about my Autrean—Spanish—side. Here I thought I was doing so well learning English, now I have to learn Spanish."

Avery chuckled. "I'm taking a Spanish class right now."

"It's hard," they said in unison, and they, even their Moeder, smiled.

"Well, this's great," Avery said, not knowing what else to say. "What a world. I had no idea."

Basil kicked a loose stone off the pathway. "A lot of us have had concerns about what's been going on, but without your help, I wouldn't have found these people. Maywood's legs and arms are getting stronger. Cameron has their medicine." Looking down at his new shoes, he stepped over and gave Avery a hug. "Thanks, for this."

"A-and us, too," Bridget said. "This's been wild for us. I never knew."

"I didn't, either," her father said shyly. "If I'd known, that night at the bar..."

Moeder Exia inhaled and wrapped her shawl over herself. She'd completely covered her face with one hand.

"N-nevertheless, I'll take care of them," he promised, "of Basil and Maywood."

At that, Basil cracked into a smile.

Avery looked over to Bridget. "I'll see you for your birthday, right?"

"I better. You and Cameron are the only ones I invited. With Maywood and Basil coming, this's the most amount of people I'll ever have at a birthday party. I was thinking of doing dirt cake. Get it, because dirt."

Avery snorted and waved them off.

Cameron had a calling with the garden animals. As they sat by the pond, sticking their finger in the water, every fish and duck would swim up to them without fail. They never nipped or splashed, they just watched them as curiously as Cameron watched them. They enjoyed them so much that since being at St. Agatha's, they must've gone through four bags of fish and duck food.

They were finally wearing their glasses with the thick lenses in them. They'd refused most of their nurses' care, but when they put on the glasses, they threw themselves on the ground and cried. Apparently they had such horrible vision, they'd never seen the individual hairs on a person's head before.

With their vision cleared, Cameron looked up to Avery. *"Hey."*

"Hi." She sat beside them on the grass. *"Did you already feed them?"*

"Yeah. They were starving." They leaned against her. *"Speak to me in English."*

"Are you ready for that?"

"No, but my teacher wants me to practice, and it's easier to talk when I'm with you."

"If it makes you feel better, I'm learning Spanish at school, and I don't like it, either. It doesn't come to me as naturally as Arkeh:nen."

"Basil was telling me that. The Bridget girl is Spanish. Sometimes she speaks it with her Fader. He really does look like Basil."

"I know." She took Cameron's hand. "Is this better?"

"...I think," they said in their best English. "It's hard to understand."

"I know."

Two of Cameron's ducks swam up to the edge of the pond. Cameron twiddled their fingers in the water, enticing them. "But I teach...others about Arkeh:na, and they want to know. That's what I worry about, I had worried about. I didn't think people would like us. Now everyone wants to know it, even though we can't go back."

"I heard they're going to try to salvage what's left of the mountain and open it up to the public for research and exploration. When that's ready, you can get back your *gemmes*."

"Good. Even though they don't work with me, I still like them."

"Yes, but you can't live there anymore, got it? You can't hide back underground."

They pouted and rolled on their butt. "I could. You never find me."

"But then you'd never see the ducks. You wouldn't see sunrises or planes. You wouldn't see me—"

"Planes!" they said with a jolt. "How scary! How do they fly? My teacher says there're people in them. She lies?"

"No, there're usually dozens of people in planes."

Cameron blew out their cheeks. "So why do they make the loud noise? How do they fly without flapping their wings like a duck?"

"I'm not sure. We should look it up sometime."

"Can we do it now? I can tell Maywood and Basil. They want to know."

"Sure." Avery opened her phone to the first selfie she and Cameron had ever taken together and searched for the right words.

Acknowledgements

First and foremost, thank you to anyone who's ever liked, reblogged, retweeted, or commented anything in relation to Arkeh:na. Your love and encouragement helped push me into publishing a book that's so close to my heart. Thank you to everyone who left critiques on the first draft and emailed me their concerns, and thank you so, so much, my Kickstarter backers, for making this book possible. I never thought I'd ever publish any of my books like this. Your pledges have given me the confidence to pursue publishing for the foreseeable future. I can't thank you enough for that.

Thank you to my family, who dealt with my obsession with spelunking and gemstones during the better parts of 2017 and 2018. Thank you, Dad, for taking me caving and hiking, and thank you, Mom and Amy, for teaching me about magic and tarot cards. Thank you, Jackson, for being my honest critique partner, and thank you, Tom and Chelsey, for your overwhelmingly kind-hearted donations to the Kickstarter.

Thank you to all my wonderful Kickstarter backers!

@punderdrone
^^ Jashan MaelJoran
Martin ^^
akimika
Alana M T
Alexandra Bohannon
Alexandra St Julien
Alisha & Jaleesa
Alyssa Warner
Amaryllis Quilliou
Amber Cartier page
Annette
Anthony Haevermaet
Anthony J. Gramuglia
Ari & Sam
Barry Raifsnider
Brenna Spence
Brianna Hyacinth
Briseis
Brynne Seabrooke
C. V. Smith
Cady Cekan
Caelum Lenchner
Carrie Burton
Chelsey Wallace
CJ Gibson
Corey Buchas
Craig L.
Craig Reynolds
D. Kleymeyer
David @ FromMyBook-shelf.com
Dawn
Dia Chappell

dinomoar
Don, Beth, & Meghan Ferris
Douglas Goad
Dustbound
Edith Henry Olenius
Edward Jackson
Fermin Serena Hortas
Fio
Fruzzo
Gabrielle Huebra
H Baxter
Hadsvich
Hannah Carter
Harley Hinze
Heather Lobitz
House Fretful
Hyper Harebell
India Gale
Inky Doodle
Iris C.
James Lucas
Jamie Perrault
Jeff Sanders
Jen Sonja
Jennifer Montgomery
Jess Draws
Jill C
Jo Ramisch
John Krugman (Hastcoat)
Jolene Bourgoin
Josh Medin
Joshua Benoit
Joshua M Dreher
Kai

Kenan
Kristin
Kylar Schaad
Kyle Čaroban
Laura Hermo
Lauren L.
Laurie Stark
Layna C.
Leah Karge
Leanna C
Leedvermaak
Leishycat
Levi Dwyer
Maddie Apples
Marissa Quinn
Mark Whitehead
Marten van der Leij
Martin D.
Mary
Matthew Beckham
Matthew Y
Meghan O'Sullivan
Mel Toeller
Mia Sierra Abbott
Michel Nguyen
Michon Pittman
Mike L.
Milo Miller
MisterSebita
Morgane Bellon
Mx Micaela Godfrey
Nana K Akom
Natasha Forrester

Campbell
Nick Harris
Nuggy Windsor
Oliver Johnson
Olivia Montoya
Owen Hammer
Paul "ilys" Symeou
Phillip A.
ProwlnJazz
Rachel H Sanders
Rea Matchett
Reid Kelly
Rhiannon Raphael
Robin D.
Rory Polanco
Rowan Sanders
Sarah Callaghan
Serena Avalar
Silvia Molina
Sophia Soll Medici Stein
Spirit Healer Mage
Stephanie Tran (@literary-reader)
T.J. Franks
Tatiana Alejandra de Castro Pérez
Tifa Robles
Tom K.
Trevor D Garner
Vanessa Bodell
YamiB.
Zemoore
Zoe Gizmo Martin

Melissa Sweeney grew up in a small farm town in Connecticut and got her B.A. in English at Central Connecticut State University in 2017. Before, during, and after that time, she drew and wrote about her characters as a dubious coping mechanism for her anxiety. She currently lives with her cat Gizmo and continues battling on which story to write next. You can follow her on Instagram (@makoninah) or on her blog *melissanovels.com*.

CPSIA information can be obtained
at www.ICGtesting.com
Printed in the USA
FFHW020624120419
51687647-57117FF